Gypsyworld

Julian F. Thompson

Gypsyworld

Henry Holt and Company · *New York*

First edition
Published by Henry Holt and Company, Inc.,
115 West 18th Street, New York, New York 10011.
Published simultaneously in Canada by Fitzhenry & Whiteside Ltd.,
91 Granton Drive, Richmond Hill, Ontario L4B 2N5.

Library of Congress Cataloging-in-Publication Data
Thompson, Julian F.
Gypsyworld / Julian F. Thompson.
Summary: Kidnapped and taken to utopian Gypsyworld by its
king and queen, a group of teenagers is tested to see how they
cope in a place where the earth and its gifts are not abused.
ISBN 0-8050-1907-3
[1. Environmental protection—Fiction. 2. Conservation of
natural resources—Fiction.] I. Title.
PZ7.T371596Gy 1992
[Fic]—dc20 92-6358

Printed in the United States of America on recycled,
acid-free paper. ∞

1 3 5 7 9 10 8 6 4 2

Acknowledgment

The author gratefully acknowledges the
inspiration and information provided by
State of the World 1990
A Worldwatch Institute Report on Progress
Toward a Sustainable Society
(W. W. Norton & Company, New York, 1990)

*For everyone who loves the planet,
and for Polly and Reggie in particular*

Gypsyworld

one

THERE WEREN'T ANY VOLUNTEERS. In fact, a lot of people thought the whole idea was totally defective— "inappropriate and irresponsible," they said.

Josip and Marina were the best ones for the job, however. People could agree on that, so they were chosen. Among the seven languages they spoke was English, and they had raised a child whom everybody liked. The job was to collect five . . . *outside* kids and bring them back. In good condition; that was a requirement. Josip and Marina were the Gypsy King and Queen, elected democratically, of course.

They were told to use whatever methods they believed were best, to get the job done right. In fact, they used two different ones.

The first of them was slightly tricky, and so Josip loved it. He'd studied what were sometimes known as "the old ways" of the Romany Gypsies, his European ancestors. Scorned and even feared by the more settled and immobile residents of towns and cities everywhere, they'd been forced to use their wits and bite back on their scruples, sometimes. In order to survive, they'd come up with . . . ways of doing business that were either clever, justified or self-protective ruses (from the gypsy point of view), or "no-good, cheating, thieving, highway robbery" (all others). Josip couldn't altogether *justify* those ancient practices (like trading off a horse with heaves while it was temporarily relieved by sugar syrup or marketing some trinkets made from baser metals as "of pure Cathayan gold"), but neither would he totally abandon them, it seemed.

A movie gave him the idea for Method One—the title of a movie that was playing almost everywhere, that summer. It was called *The Gypsies,* much to his delight. But it didn't have a thing to do with Josip and Marina, or any of their ancestors, or relatives, or friends.

Instead, it was about four *cowboys,* from Wyoming, handsome but naive straight-shooters from the sticks who, feeling that their lives were awfully short of "females and excitement," decided they would move to New York City. There, they bought and operated four unlicensed taxicabs, and had a lot of violent fun, while meeting girls and taming wildlife in the urban jungle. The movie was extremely popular, with all the different age groups.

But anyway, what Josip did, the week before that movie came to town, was run some big display ads in the local paper, in the entertainment section. Here's what they said, in bold, black letters:

SELL YOUR KID TO THE GYPSIES

Most people figured there must be a misprint in the ad. They thought that it was *meant* to say: "SEND YOUR KID TO . . ."—you know, see the movie. Other, more sophisticated readers said the ad was clever and "a real eye-catcher."

But there also were a few, as Josip and Marina had been

sure there'd be, who read the ad and raised their eyebrows and said, "Hmmm." And even licked their lips, right after that.

♦ ♦ ♦

In order to make sure they'd have a chance to meet some members of this group of people, Josip drove the Winnebago into different parts of town. And every time he parked the thing, he hung a big cloth sign that covered half the side of it. The sign had just two words on it: THE GYPSIES.

With that accomplished, Josip and Marina would then stand outside the big RV and do a little puttering around— like, cleaning chrome, or washing windows. They'd also smile at passersby, and tell them "Howdy."

Some of those addressed would stop and chat. A few of them were fellow Winnebago owners. Others would be folks with nothing else to do. But in every neighborhood, almost, there also would be one who'd look around and kind of force a little laugh, and say, "You know—there was an ad here, in the paper, just the other day . . ."

And half the time that person would end up inside the van and talking business, talking numbers, talking *turkey*. Negotiations would begin, in other words.

Josip and Marina found the best buys were in just the makes and models they were after: male and female *teenage* kids. Before the day was done, they'd shaken hands on deals for two or three of them.

♦ ♦ ♦

Once a deal had been agreed upon, Josip and Marina would hand the seller something in a small white envelope. Not

♦ 3 ♦

what you are thinking—no, not yet. It was a level teaspoon-ful of finely ground up roots and herbs, a compound that, in bygone days, was called by different names in different countries. To gypsies back in Wales, the stuff was known as *Bighnow;* Spanish gypsies used to label it *Adios, muchachas* (Josip had been told). By any name, this blend could put an ox to sleep for up to fourteen hours.

The sellers' job would be to stir it into something in the icebox they were pretty sure the kid would eat or drink, when she or he came in the house. The compound didn't have a color, taste or odor.

Once the sleeping body was transported to the van, the sellers would be paid, in crisp new twenty-dollar bills. The money would be fake-o—counterfeit—of course, but not because the King and Queen were cheap. Oh, no, no, no. They did that for the sake of . . . history, to more or less commemorate "the old ways." And besides, it was a "just desserts" type deal, in their opinion.

Those parents were, they felt, the kind you wouldn't want to buy a used *car* from, let alone a kid who they'd been driving up a wall, the past twelve years, or more.

But still, they did buy two or three—the number doesn't matter.

♦   ♦   ♦

In order to fill out the group of five, Josip and Marina used their second method. It was terribly old fashioned, and it might have been "authentic," but they weren't sure of that. What they *were* sure of was that it worked, and fast. They just *took* the ones they wanted, kids they'd noticed walking by themselves, along some totally deserted street. They'd knock them out with chloroform, for ease in handling.

Doing this was not a thing the King and Queen were proud of, not at all. But they convinced themselves it was essential to the . . . well, experiment. To include some kids who might be sort of *average,* in terms of what their parents thought of them. Maybe the kids they stole would even be *superior.*

"Hey," said Josip, with a laugh, "I take that chance."

two

"Is anybody thirsty?" asked Marina, cheerfully.

The van was parked, all by itself, in one far corner of a campground. She and Josip were relaxing in the two big imitation-leather swivel chairs, the one the driver of a Winnebago sits in, and the one right next to it. They'd unlocked the swivels and had turned the chairs around, so as to face the kids. All five of them were lying on their bunks, in dark blue sleeping bags. They were all awake, just lying there and talking.

This talking took the form of questions and complaints, addressed to one another and the King and Queen. And it was loud. Josip was a little tired of it.

"Everybody! Hey!" he said. "You want to bring yourselves to order? Sshhh." They got a little quieter. "You'll get your questions answered by and by. But, first off—who would like some iced tea or some soda?"

At fifty-eight, Josip was a tall, strong barrel of a man, dark complected, with a great crag of a nose, and an elastic, full-lipped mouth that, smiling, showed a lot of large, square teeth. His hair, a salt-and-pepper mix, was dense beyond belief, shiny with good health (and just a dab of

Vaseline), neatly trimmed and combed without a part. He wore safari clothes: a tan bush jacket with a belt and epaulets, matching trousers stuffed into the tops of soft black boots. His hands were huge, and active.

The question that he'd asked brought answers from the kids. All of them said "Me," or "I would," and two of them, from habit, stuck a finger up, outside their sleeping bags.

Josip smiled, said, "Yes! Outstanding!" He nodded at Marina, and the two of them stood up and went to the refrigerator. They took out a pitcher of iced tea and an enormous soda bottle. Then, each of them put glasses on a tray and went from bed to bed. Josip offered the iced tea, Marina passed the soda.

The Queen, a graceful server, looked to be a little younger than her husband. Her hair was all dark copper, the color of neglected cookware, and it tumbled to her shoulders in rambunctious, heavy waves. She had a broad nose on a round and merry face, which featured perfect buckwheat-honey skin, and teeth as white and even as a show dog's. Her body seemed robust: full breasts above a slender waist, roundly solid, energetic hips. That day, she wore a flowered rayon blouse, its top three buttons left undone, and a swirling, full black skirt that showed her shapely calves above a pair of narrow red suede boots.

Each kid took a glass and drank. All their arms were bare; their shoulders, too. All of them had woven silver bracelets on one wrist.

Josip and Marina sat back down again. He sighed. Neither of them had taken anything to drink. The kids put down their empty glasses on the floor beside their bunks. Now, instead of normal talking, yelling and the like, they began to speak in tiny little *whispers*. Josip and Marina looked at one another.

"Here is an improvement," Josip said. "Now, is possible to talk. Marina and myself to talk. And not to worry, everyone, this small disablement is very temporary thing." He cupped one ear, so as to hear a whisper from the right side of the van.

"Yes," he said. "Exactly right. Was something in the drinks, correct. *Shadoop,* they called it in Romania—decoction made from steeping certain barks in fresh spring water. Paralyzes vocal cords a little while—but be as good as ever, by and by."

"We give you this *shadoop,*" Marina added, "for multiple good reasons, starting with: No interruptions. But other ones as well, believe you me."

"So, now," said Josip, "we address the questions in your minds. One by one by one."

"Who are us? you wonder," said Marina. "And I tell you, right straight out. He is Josip. *Jo-sip,*" she repeated, slowly. "Gypsy King. I am wife to him, Mah-ree-nah, Gypsy Queen." She smiled at the expressions on their faces. "Absolutely true. No stuff."

Her husband waved and bowed to all five kids in turn, as if acknowledging her introduction.

"Second question," he announced. "Is of extremely great importance, yes? Where the heck my clothes? I mean by that, of course, *your* clothes. No doubt you noticed you're not wearing any."

"We have them put away," Marina said. "And in a day or two, we give them back to you, and new ones, too."

"We took them off you for two reasons," Josip said. "The first one is: Security. Reason number two is just as good, but I can't tell you it. You'll see, I think. Later on, you'll understand, I bet."

By this time, all five kids were looking at each other with

expressions on their faces that included one or more of these: stupefaction, panic, fury and frustration. Fear.

"You're wondering where is the bathroom," said Marina, getting up. "Is right back here." She walked on through the van and opened up a narrow gray door in the back.

"And also maybe wondering," her husband said, "how you will get there, without clothes. Well, don't worry. Has been done, I promise you."

"We keep all lights down low," Marina said. "And thanks to the *shadoop* no one makes remarks, you see? Bodies nothing you should be ashamed of, anyway. Lots worse things than naked. No one's perfect, right? Everybody different."

"Now, on to other questions," boomed the King. "Here's a biggie: How come you got here, to this van? Everybody wants to know that baby."

"Answer," said Marina, "is: Two different ways. Some of you, your parents sold you to us. Honest. Others, we just stole. And no, you never going to know which which is which."

"Now," said Josip to Marina. "Names. More names." He faced the kids again. "You know that we are Josip and Marina. Now is time to name the names of other members of the family. The names we call the five of you, when we adopted you."

He saw the looks on different faces.

"Hey, but maybe not forever," he added. "Possibly be up to you."

"Oh, yes," Marina said. "All of you now got *new* names. You've noticed that already, right? Read them on the ID bracelets that you're wearing, that you can't get off, I bet."

"The oldest one of you," the King said, grandly, "gets the honored letter A, the first one. He is Alec, over there. Grand old man of seventeen."

He pointed to a boy who had a narrow face and blondish-reddish curly hair. His hairstyle was an Afro, but it needed combing. He stared back at the King.

"Next oldest—she sixteen—is B for Brenda," said the Queen. She smiled and made a graceful, palm-up gesture at the black girl who was lying on her back, and shaking her head, as if in disbelief. She looked over at the Queen and rolled her eyes around.

"Carrie's in the middle, at the age of *fifteen*," Josip then contributed. He wiggled his fingers at a brown-haired girl who had actually been lying with her head propped on one hand, and both bare shoulders showing, and the top part of her chest. She stuck her tongue out at the King, then made a pistol of her hand and shot him.

"Dennis is fourteen," Marina jumped back in to say, "the second to the youngest." The boy had jet-black hair and eyebrows, and skin the color of the Queen's. Carefully, he mouthed two words at her, neither of them *Your* or *Majesty*. Marina laughed at him. He turned away and faced the wall.

"And finally, let me introduce Elizabeth, the youngest in the family," said Josip. He nodded toward the girl whose bunk was closest to his wife. "She's going to be thirteen in three days' time. We have to have a party."

Elizabeth had straight black hair that was parted in the middle. Her large, brown almond eyes were seen to glisten in the twilight, and her body made the smallest mound by far, inside her sleeping bag.

"Three final questions for today," Marina said. "First one: Why the heck *do* Josip and Marina pick up Alec, Brenda, Carrie, Dennis and Elizabeth, and put them in a Winnebago van? Second: Just how long, exactly, must they have to stay?"

"Answer one," said Josip. "We have pick you up—

collected you—for dam' good reason, possibly the best there is. Answer number two: A while." He laughed at the expression—nausea? disgust?—on Alec's face. "Pair of crummy answers, right, big A?" The boy did not reply.

"Question third and last," Marina said. "Where Josip and Marina taking these five kids?" She cocked her head toward her husband and shrugged her shoulders, much as if she didn't know herself.

A huge smile stretched across his face. He spread his arms apart, as if embracing all the earth.

"Gypsyworld, of course," he said. "Best answer possible."

three

AT DIFFERENT TIMES, that night, everyone slipped out of his or her blue sleeping bag and tiptoed to the bathroom. Carrie watched them all, making no attempt to hide what she was doing. Others probably did too (given all the reasons that they had to lie awake), but Josip and Marina, looking in their rearview mirrors, couldn't tell for sure. It was too dim inside the van for them to see whose eyes were closed, and whose were slitted open.

The King and Queen kept driving all night long. They drove at fifty-five, or sometimes fifty. Their motor home was very quiet, for a Winnebago van. Shortly after dawn, they turned onto the bridge that headed up and out to Gypsy-world.

For years and years—indeed, for generations—that same bridge had been available to gypsies, moving into Gypsy-world, but not to other people. Other people didn't know that it was there. It was made in such a way they couldn't see it, yet.

four

THE WINNEBAGO STOPPED, and Josip turned the
motor off. He stretched his arms above his head, with both
fists clenched, and roared, as follows: "AHHrrr." Most people would have said it was a sound of celebration and relief,
of victory, thanksgiving, even.

He turned around and peered into the dimness of the van.

"We're home," he told his riders, smiling broadly.

Marina nodded and undid her seat belt. Then she stood
and came around her seat, to burrow in a storage area built
in behind it.

"To celebrate," she said, "let's everybody get their
clothes, again."

One by one, she picked up little piles of folded clothing,
and carried them to one bunk or another, five in all. She put
each pile down on a person's stomach, there or right beside
it, on the bed. Everyone got running shoes, or high-topped
court shoes.

"We're going in," said Josip. "Please to join us, when
you're ready."

He got up and left the van, Marina following. The door
swung shut behind them.

"Oh, sure," said Carrie.

"Well, at least we've got our clothes and voices back," said Brenda. "And I don't see the point of staying in this motor home . . ."

What followed was a lot of rustling and hustling and bustling. Only Carrie got completely out of bed before she started dressing; only small Elizabeth got *all* her clothes on while inside her sleeping bag.

Dennis didn't even tie his shoes before he ran around and pulled up all the shades.

It was a sunny day, and everyone could see that they were in a driveway, and beside a house. The house was not exactly usual. It seemed to be two stories high, with a slanty, shingled roof—except it had a turret in one corner, with a battlement on top of it. The building looked as if it might be made of poured concrete, and it was painted blue and white. That is to say, the bottom floor was painted white, the second floor a nice pale blue, and the turret those two colors, candy striped. On one side of the house, there was an all-glass bubble of a porch, a big one. Even its whole roof was glass, and it seemed full of houseplants, some of them as tall as corn. Brenda even thought that some of them *resembled* corn, or what she thought corn looked like. The only times she'd seen the stuff, except for ears or cans of it, had been on television.

Through the window on the other side, the kids could see two neighbors' houses. Although different colored and without a turret, they were shaped a good deal like the King and Queen's. Both of them had glassed-in porches and pitched roofs with rows of those same funny-looking shingles on them. They also had nice gardens in their yards, and what appeared to be a pair of small, aboveground pools, not really big enough to swim in. Brenda had the feeling it was very bright outside, and vivid, *different:* the greens of all the vegetation, the colors of the houses, and the clouds and sky (what little she could see of them). This Gypsyworld appeared to her a good deal like the picture on a really great TV set: sharp and clean and clear. Lifelike, only better.

The street was lined with leafy trees, but it was not well traveled, at this time of day, at least. It seemed to be the sort of street you'd find in what would be the *nicer* part of town; the atmosphere was peaceful. A double-decker bus passed by, but quietly, discreetly. There wasn't any advertising on the side of it.

"Well," said Alec. "They've abandoned us, apparently. Joe Zip and the boat dock." He'd been peering out the windows on both sides, but as he spoke he turned around, perhaps to see if anyone had gotten that. It turned out he wore glasses, aviator style, and was quite tall. When he'd gotten all his stuff back from the Queen, he'd combed his Afro out. He liked to tell kids in his class he planned to be a famous novelist, like Salinger or Pynchon; few of them had heard of either one. And although in his heart he knew he'd never make it as a writer (or as anything important or worthwhile), he'd also heard that Einstein had been terrible at math, in school.

"They both went inside the house, just like they said," said Brenda. "You didn't hear them say that?" She'd never much admired white kids who affected Afros. She thought that they looked unbelievable, like black third graders dressed in Pilgrims' clothes.

"It's not a *house*," said Carrie, giggling. "This'd have to be the *palace,* wouldn't it?" She fluffed her hair in back.

Carrie's hair was barely shoulder length, frizzed out. Her

clothes were tight white jeans, a T-shirt, black, with *Uzi-Buzi* on the front of it in wide pink script, and a faded denim jacket over that. Anyone who'd watched her getting dressed was perfectly aware her chunky roundness didn't have a thing to do with flab.

Carrie liked to think that in a former life she'd been a movie actress. Marilyn Monroe. And when she'd read a piece about the star, while waiting in a supermarket checkout line, she knew she *felt* like her, as well. In other words, she felt both glamorous and . . . well, *uncertain* of herself, sometimes. She felt beyond her wildest dreams and one big nightmare. Her one accomplishment was that she'd learned piano on her own and played by ear.

"Roger willco, right, uh-huh—a palace." Alec nodded three times, up and down. He laughed, but not good humoredly. "Of course—the *palace*."

"Hey, check the door there, guy," said Dennis. "Could be they left it open, still."

"Check it your own self, amigo," Alec said. "I don't see it making that much difference, either way."

Dennis looked up at him. He'd dropped down on one knee, to get his high-tops tied, and he felt *coiled*. He could imagine just *exploding* up from there (like, ZOOM!), his right arm straight and ending in a rock-hard fist which made connections (POW!) with that tall gringo's jaw. He'd "amigo" him. Teach *him* to mess. He wore black jeans and a bright red muscle-T. His body was developed, for fourteen.

It seemed to him that maybe—possibly, *conceivably*—this was the first chance that he'd ever had in all his life to do a major thing that *he* decided, that he *chose*. To be, for once, a little like his dad, the man they used to call *El Torbellino*, yes, the Whirlwind, once upon a time the roughest fighter, pound for pound (he'd read this in a clipping that his mother had) ever to come out of Lupo's gym.

"If that door ain't locked, I'm takin' off," he said. "I'm outa here, I'm gone, I'm history. I'm ho-ome free. I'll be back there with my homeboys 'fore you know it."

That was a joke. He didn't have no homeboys. His folks had kept him out of any gang, of any trouble, any fun—hey, of any *anything* but school and stocking shelves and coolers at Joe's Discount Beverages, his father's place of business, nowadays. That was what they called his father, now, "Hey, Joe . . ." *He* called him "Dad," or "sir," and did *exactly* what he said, or else. His father and his mother, both, enforced "the rules"—no hanging out, no girls, work at the store, mostly in the back (stacking cases made him strong, at least), homework checked each morning, early bedtime, and repeat. On vacation, work all day. They'd decided he would be a doctor or a lawyer, one.

Now he swung his head to look at each of those four others.

"What gives here? Aren't you, like, *with* me?" He stared at Brenda. "Aren't *you?*"

She shrugged. Brenda's mother'd told her many times that she was a *direct* descendant of the valiant François Dominique Toussaint L'Ouverture (*"Fran-swa, Doe-min-eek, Too-san, Louver-toor,"* her mother always said), who, in the late 1700s, became the fighting father of Haitian independence. Toussaint, though black, had had some French blood in his veins as well, and there were few things *Frenchier* (so Brenda thought) than big, long shoulder shrugs.

"Which way you going to go?" she said.

"*Any* way," the boy replied. "What the hell's the diff? We

can hitch a ride, I bet. Or even find a cop. Get a little *law* in this. Say, we been *kidnapped,* man. *Some* of us have been. I bet we're on TV, already."

He could stand that, being on TV. That'd get him some respect at school, next year, and walking down the street, from someone other than the teachers and the nerds. He was sure that *he'd* been stolen, kidnapped. His parents had big plans for him. "You gonna make us proud of you, or die in the attempt," his father'd told him once, just before he put the belt to him, "showing that he loves you," as his mother always said. Of course it was *conceivable* his dad and mom had gotten so disgusted they had given up on him. He'd forgotten he was meant to set up the chairs for the Ladies Sodality meeting in the church hall, the Saturday before; that had been right up there on the edge of unforgivable.

"I wouldn't be so sure," said Brenda, and she sat down on her bunk, again, the very edge of it, hands folded on her knees, which, like her feet, were close together, touching. She wished she'd put on pumps, that day, instead of running shoes, but still she thought she looked all right. She was slender and high waisted, wearing stylish, pleated olive pants, narrow down below the knee, and an oversize gold shirt, with five black buttons at the neck. Her kinky chestnut hair was long, and drawn straight back, secured into a ponytail by yellow velvet ribbon. Her face was like a cat's, with a stubby nose and wide-set eyes, and a slightly pointed chin. Her skin was light mahogany in color, and she wore two silver bracelets and three rings. Every time her mother told her who she was descended from, she asked her when she planned to start to get the sort of grades she *should be* getting, with the lineage she had.

"I've never seen a place that looked like this, before," she added. Then, more darkly, "I wouldn't be so sure that you can *get* back to your home—*chez vous*—from here."

Brenda flicked her eyes toward Alec, after saying that. He was the only one of those four kids who looked as if he *could* be taking French. The others looked like pure vo-tech, except for maybe what's-her-face—Elizabeth—the little Asian-looking one. A lot of Asians were really good in school, especially in math, or with *computers*. If no one else had taken any French but her, she could speak a lot of it, the next few days. She liked the way it sounded, even when she didn't get the words just right.

Dennis was standing up by then. He pushed a palm at Brenda. It was a gesture of disgust, and of dismissal. (GET LOST! DROP DEAD! GET OUTA HERE!)

"That makes a real whole lot of sense," he said. He tried the door; it swung right open. Now he looked at Carrie.

Awake and sleeping, he had dreamed of someday meeting, knowing, maybe *rescuing* a girl who looked like Carrie. He would do anything for her. When they got older, he would buy her all the clothes she'd ever want, a nice house in the canyons, out of town, and jewelry, a sports car of her own. Now, at this present age, he'd simply like to hold her. Yes, and *kiss* her, too. He'd never touched a girl in any way at all, except for shaking hands. His father's rules, again. Girls could get a boy in trouble, so his father said.

"Okay, gorgeous, let's make tracks," he said to her. It seemed as if his normal speaking voice was hoarse. In fact, he yelled a lot, at home, sometimes in the cellar, being beaten by his dad, but much more often in his room. He might be doing homework when he'd suddenly get up and go and flop face forward on his bed, and jam his face into his pillow, and just scream.

Carrie bit down on a corner of her lip, and looked from out the door to him, and back again. She'd shot a hip out and she had her hand on it. The article had said that Marilyn's real hair was nowhere near as blond as in the pictures that you saw of her. She hadn't answered Dennis, but she was pretty sure he got the message she was sending, that she wasn't going with him.

Dennis turned to Alec, next. "Hey! You're comin'—right, big fella?"

The tall boy ambled over to the door.

"I'm torn," he said. "On the one hand . . . well, it *does* look different here—bizarre. What did Joe Zip call it? *Gypsyworld?* I'll tell you this much: I thought that those two *looked* like gypsies."

"Yeah, and don't forget that stuff we had to drink." Carrie made a face, forgetting that it didn't have a taste at all. "Yucky-*poo.* I know darn good and well my mom has never heard of anything along *those* lines. If she had, she would have bought it by the case. She would have put it in my *bottle.*" She pursed her lips and made some sucking sounds, then went and sat down on her bunk and crossed her legs and then her arms, below her breasts.

Dennis was standing in the open door and facing them. He hit the doorjamb with his fist (KABOOM!).

"What's the matter with you *jerks*?" he said. "We may be runnin' out of time! Those gypsy mothuhs might come back and zap us any minute—knock us out and lock us up for good. Let us *rot,* somewhere. So, look, I'm going now. Who's coming with me? You—Elizabeth!" he shouted at the little girl. She was still inside her sleeping bag. "You want to come?"

She reminded him a little of this skinny, half-grown cat he'd seen one day, crouched in the weeds outside a boarded-up old house between his place and school. It had fled at his approach, but he had left some tuna fish out of his luncheon sandwich near the place where he had seen it. And the next day, too, and the one after that. Coming home from school the fourth day, he had seen the cat again, but lying in the street, right by the curb. He guessed it must have been run over.

Elizabeth continued saying nothing, but she looked at Brenda. *She* was staring off into a distant corner of the van, ignoring Dennis altogether. She was practicing some words inside her head, like *Montparnasse.* The little girl began to shake her head.

"I wouldn't say there's any tearing rush to go," said Alec. "I'm not sure they plan to lock us up at all. It's just a hunch I have, a feeling, like, a *sensibility*—but I don't think so. I sense another plot line here, so me, I'm going to check things out a little more, before I make *my* move." His eyes went once around the room, but furtively. Then he stuck his hands into the pockets of his jeans and went and peered out of the window on the other side, opposite the door.

Dennis made a quick disgusted sound (PATOOEY!).

"To hell with all of you," he said. "Dumb buncha chicken livers. I wouldn't take you with me if you begged me to. As far as I'm concerned, you all can stay here till you *rot!*"

With that, he made a strangled sound and jumped right out the door, and thereby disappeared. Brenda was pretty sure she recognized the sound for what it was, a sob. The little tough guy'd made his exit, crying.

"Good riddance," Alec said, with gusto. "Dumb little greaser. Now the rest of us can come to an intelligent decision . . ."

"*Right,*" said Carrie, sulkily. Dennis had been kind of cute. And he had called her "gorgeous." "By listening to you? I bet you wouldn't call that kid a greaser to his face."

"May I pose a question?" Brenda said. "I'm curious." She had a twinkle in her big dark eyes. "How many of you think you *know* your parents didn't sell you, like that *M'sieur* Josip said?"

"Well," said Alec, instantly, "I'd have to say that I doubt *very* much my folks would do a thing like that, even as some kind of joke, or something. Now I'm not saying that my father thinks I'm . . . well, the offspring of his dreams, a superson, or anything like that." (How had he put it, actually—"You everlasting *nincompoop*"?) "But no, they wouldn't sell me to some strangers, I don't think. I mean, I'm *sure* of that."

"And me," said Carrie, pouting still, "*my* mother always calls me 'precious.' She would never, ever sell me to some gypsies." She paused as if to think the matter over, give it her best shot. And then her whole face brightened, and she smiled. "It could be *you*, you know," she said to Brenda. "Did you ever think of that? For all you know, you could have been, like, Special of the Week." She giggled.

"*Impossible,*" said Brenda, giving it the French pronunciation. She thought that it was great they had some words spelled just the same as English.

"Well, how about Elizabeth?" said Carrie, and she laughed again. "Except they wouldn't want to sell her by the pound." No doubt about it, she was on a roll; that happened.

There was a sniffle from the dimness of the small girl's bunk.

"Now look what you done," said Brenda. "That wasn't very nice." She put her hand beside her mouth, as if to shout great distances. "It's all right, Elizabeth. Carrie's only joking. You be cool." But when the sniffles didn't stop, she shrugged again.

Alec paced across the room and took his third look out the door. His running shoes were much the most athletic part of him. Even walking, he was poorly balanced, awkward. ("Clumsy lummox" was the way his father often put it.)

"*I* think what we might do at this point is go on inside," he said, "and try to get a . . . yes, a handle on the situation. See if we can find out who these people really are, exactly— them and anybody else who lives here. And find out what they plan to do with us."

"*Magnifique!*" said Brenda. "What a strategy! I *totally* agree with you!" And Alec beamed until she went on in a different tone of voice. "Seeing as my other choice is sitting in this house-on-wheels and listening to her"—she tossed her head out toward the sniffling—"and 'Precious,' here." She laughed. "Seems to me I *said* we should go in, right after Josip and Marina left."

She stood up and checked her hair, and started for the door. Alec, who'd been standing right beside it, saw her coming, and he jumped out first, ahead of her, landing with a thump. Brenda stopped and looked back toward the little girl, who still was lying there, inside her sleeping bag.

"Elizabeth," she said. Her voice got down to business. "Come on. Get out of bed and come with me. I may not be the Secret Service or the U.S. Cavalry, but you're a damn sight better off with me than by yourself, in here."

The little girl sat up and did as she was told. She was wearing wrinkled drawstring pants that were a sort of eggshell color (and were not too clean), and a big green sweatshirt with its sleeves rolled up enough so that they didn't hide her hands. It could almost slip right off one shoulder. Her chest was flat as Dennis's, but her finely featured face was delicately feminine. She also looked completely cowed and hopeless, like a small wild bird, too young to fly, which also has been touched too much, by children. When she got out of her bunk and came into the light, it was clear she was part Asian, just as Brenda'd thought.

Elizabeth knew her mother'd brought her to this country, using money that her father's parents sent her. She knew that all of them, except the father, met one time at a hotel. And after that her father's parents took her from her mother, and got into their car, and drove away. She'd never seen her father, or her mother, after that. Her father's father was quite senile. He sometimes called the child "the Dragon Lady." When she asked her grandmother how come she lived with them, the woman said they'd found her in a cabbage patch.

As soon as Brenda'd seen that she was up, she'd gone on out the door. Carrie jumped out, too, before Elizabeth could get to it.

◆　◆　◆

Alec was standing looking at the house's big front door. It was pale blue; there wasn't any bell. As the others came up close, he knocked on it, three times. There wasn't any answer right away, and so he looked around, his hand still made into a fist, and shifted weight from one foot to the other.

Then, suddenly, the door swung open, and Marina smiled at them.

"You should have walked right in," she said. "It wasn't locked, you know. It never is."

They followed her into an entryway. A wooden staircase right in front of them led to the second floor. On their right, there was a beaded curtain that Marina went through, saying, "Come."

That put them in the living room. It was large and cluttered, comfortable. Glass doors on one side opened on the porch—or, possibly, solarium—the one they'd seen from the outside. Across the room there was a fireplace that had a soapstone stove in front of it. Heavy draw drapes flanked the sliding doors, and there were big fat cushions on the floor, as well as two upholstered chairs, a curving damask-covered sofa, and a giant dark red Barcalounger that the King was sitting on. The room had lots of highly polished wooden tables in it, and on the tops of them were wooden boxes, carvings, multicolored geodes—even one clear crystal ball, sitting on a wooden saucer made of polished ebony. Pictures on the walls were landscapes and still lifes, as well as some abstracts. There were also portraits: bearded men and smiling women, some of them with halos, or a babe in arms. To one side of the mantel was a giant globe, held in a wooden stand; it was a good two feet across, at the equator. The bookcase right beside it very nearly reached the ceiling and was stuffed with volumes, old and new. Brenda saw they had *Les Misérables*. In one corner was a grand piano. The bulbs in all the lamps were strangely shaped.

"So—here you are," said Josip, warmly, to the group. "Welcome, welcome, welcome. And I bet you're hungry, yes? Soon, we will sit down and eat." He gestured toward the far end of the room, and made some scooping motions with his hand. Delicious cooking smells came wafting through the air.

"Mmm," said Brenda, "sure smells *good*." She smiled, hoping what she'd said had covered up the gurgle sounds that she could feel her stomach making.

"Do—please—sit down," Marina said, "and make yourselves at home." She settled on a brocade-covered cushion, tailor fashion, and she watched the group find places to sit down. No one joined her on the floor.

"I'm only seeing four of you," she added. "Is no Dennis."

"No," said Alec, promptly. "Dennis ran away. He hopes to make it home. Or go to the police. Or see himself on television." He laughed, but stopped at once when Carrie looked at him.

"Don' worry, he be back," said Josip, sounding altogether unconcerned. "Here is only home for him, for now. He'll see."

Alec cleared his throat. "But where *is* here, exactly?" he inquired. "We've been wondering. This doesn't look like anywhere we've been, before."

"Is not," the Gypsy King replied. "I told you that. Is Gypsyworld."

"Gypsyworld?" repeated Brenda. "Me, I've heard of Disneyworld. That's down in Florida. Our neighbor went there, once; she thought that it was neat. Is this like *that*, at all?"

Josip and Marina laughed.

"Not really, no," she said. "Disneyworld is fantasy; Gypsyworld is possible. Only one Walt Disney, but a lot of gypsies."

"Who are gypsies?" said a tiny voice. "I don't know that word."

All eyes traveled to the sofa, where Elizabeth was sitting—she at one end, Brenda at the other. No one had ever heard her speak, before.

Marina smiled. "We gypsies, my dear child," she gently said, "we *small*-g gypsies, we are every kind of people. Some few of us are big-G Gypsies, too, descended from the constant wanderers who came from India, to start with, and then spread around through Europe, Asia and, more lately, North America. But basically, and here in Gypsyworld, we're all the same, all small-g gypsies, drawn from different races, tribes of people; travelers from everywhere and every nation in the whole wide world."

"Between us, we have seen all kinds of happenings, all rights and wrongs," her husband added solemnly. "We've seen the samenesses and differences in every race of people, and our blood is now a mix of every kind of blood. Gypsyworld, you see, is growing, even to this day. We learn of people, many every year, on Earth—*your* Earth—who have been seeking Gypsyworld. We get in touch with them, and show them how to come."

"The people here"—his wife, once more, took up the explanation—"are simply those who've come to see, and celebrate, the point." She dropped her head and it was quiet in the room.

"The *point?*" said Alec. His voice seemed extra loud, and this time all the other kids looked over at him. "I mean, what's *that* mean, anyway?" It was clear to everyone that he was blushing. "*What* point? The point of what?"

"I can answer all those questions," said the Gypsy Queen, still softly, looking up at him with great affection. Brenda, seeing that, could not believe her eyes. She stared, in total fascination, at the Queen.

"But you will never understand the answers," she went on. "Not until you have no need to ask the questions, anymore."

"End of conversation," Josip said, while getting up. "Now is *surely* time to eat."

five

❧

THEIR MEAL CONSISTED of hot loaves of aromatic whole grain bread, which Josip cut in big thick slices, and then served along with bowls of much the thickest spicy soup that any of the kids had ever eaten. Alec wondered what he'd call it, if he kept a journal; it probably was *goulash*, he decided. Brenda tried to think what *vichyssoise* consisted of. Josip suggested they would want to "democratically decide" the question of which rooms the four of them would occupy. They could do that when the meal was over, maybe.

"All second floor is yours," he said. "Marina and myself sleep back down there." He pointed to a little hall beyond the dining area. "I don' like to be a long ways from the kitchen." And he laughed and slapped his solid center with both open hands.

So, when everyone had finished eating, Alec, Brenda, Carrie and Elizabeth trooped up the stairs, together. None of them had said the soup was good, but all of them had eaten second helpings when Marina offered them, and the oldest two had said "Yes, please" and "*Oui, merci*," while holding out their bowls. They weren't asked to help clean up, after the meal, and no one volunteered.

"I wonder what was in that stuff," said Carrie, once the four of them were out of earshot. "Watch all our hair fall out, or something." She yanked on her left eyebrow, but it seemed to be secure.

"I can't see why they'd want to drug us *now,*" said Brenda. "Seems like, now they'd want us *sharp,* so maybe we could get that *point* she talked about."

That hadn't made a lot of sense, to her. Brenda'd *played* "the point"—point guard—on JV basketball, at school, her sophomore year. But now she knew the kind of point Marina'd been referring to had more to do with heavy stuff, like life and happiness. Understanding it would surely be a problem, she believed. Among the things that Brenda didn't get the point *of,* there was algebra, in school.

"Was that *peculiar?*" Alec asked. "Or what? I'm meant to understand some 'point,' or find out what it *is,* when they won't even tell me where I am, or what I'm meant to do, or why they got me in the first place? What do they think I am? Some kind of genius?"

"We-ell," said Carrie, instantly, "if I were you, I wouldn't sweat *that* possibility too much. Josip and Marina may be gypsies, but they aren't *morons,* necessarily . . ."

"So—here's the bathroom," Brenda said. She was looking through the first door on the right, there on the second floor. She didn't want to listen to a lot of bickering. But she, herself, was curious. What *did* Josip and Marina really think of Alec? Marina'd looked at him as if she really *liked* him. That made Brenda wonder. Was she missing something?

Not too likely, no; she didn't think she was. Alec wasn't like *quadratics,* complicated, hard to get. You didn't have to dig or sweat to understand what he was all about. The guy was not some Shakespeare dude. He was probably all right, just awful *geeky*. Wanted to be something big, but maybe never would be, even if you gave him bonus lifetimes, left him on the line forever.

Everybody stood there, staring at the bathroom. It was a big one, but it had no tub—just a nice tiled shower in one corner, and a toilet (in its own compartment, with a door), and a lot of towels on racks, and a pair of straight-backed chairs and, yes, twin sinks, that his-and-hers arrangement.

"Ooh, how chummy," Carrie said, and pointed. There were five different-colored toothbrushes, hanging on a rack between the sinks. "Anybody want to do their teeth with me?"

Alec looked around the room with eyebrows raised, simulating great indifference. He had assumed that everyone had seen him naked in the van (and not *just* Carrie), just as he had seen the four of them (although pretending not to have). But that didn't mean that he was ready to be part of, like, a *commune* of some sort. He was the oldest and the only guy, but he wasn't all that . . . carefree. He could guess what kind of comments Carrie'd make, if she was capable of speech and saw him standing in that shower, there. He checked the bathroom door. It looked as if there was a working lock on it. When his eyes came up from doing that, they ran into Elizabeth's.

The bedrooms were all different. One was much the biggest. It went from front to back, on one side of the house. It contained a king-size bed that had a mirror for a headboard, two cushioned maple chairs, a desk with chair, a little couch that looked convertible, and an enormous walk-in closet.

A second room was in the tower, so it naturally was round, and had extremely narrow windows, and the pictures hanging on the wall looked funny. But its most outstanding feature was the bed; it actually was heart shaped! Brenda laughed when she caught sight of it, and Alec blushed. Carrie went and sat on it, and jiggled up and down until it squeaked. Elizabeth just stood there looking mystified.

"*Magnifique*," said Brenda, and she knew that other people noticed.

Of the two remaining rooms, one was very small and plain. It contained a single bed, a chest that had four drawers in it, a clothes rack, and a small upholstered chair.

"*I* know who gets *this* one," Carrie said, as she looked into it.

The final room looked like a *guest* room, Brenda thought. The curtains matched the bedspread, and there was a luggage rack, and four books on the bedside table, three of which looked lousy. The fourth one was a cartoon book.

They all went back out to the hall again.

Elizabeth spoke up. "I want the little room," she said. "I know I'm going to get it anyway, so"—she paused and seemed to think—"so, what's the diff? But I just thought I'd tell you that. I *want* it."

"You sure of that, Elizabeth?" said Brenda, right away. Although she didn't think she gave a hoot which room the little girl was in—and she *was* the youngest, after all—she felt she had to keep on standing up for her. A little, anyway. Just because . . . well, *someone* ought to.

"I'm sure," Elizabeth replied, with great conviction, and she went and stood right in the small room's door. "This *is* my room," she told them all, defiantly.

"Okay with me," said Carrie. She looked at Brenda and at

Alec. "How 'bout we raffle off the other ones? Throw fingers and count off? You know that way? We'll start with Alec, right? Okay? On three?"

Carrie won, and whooped, and chose the heart-shaped bed. Alec then announced he didn't care, that he'd let Brenda take her choice of the remaining two. She took the guest room look-alike, which left him with the biggest one.

"That means you get to room with Dennis," Carrie told him, gleefully.

Alec winced. "I guess," he said. "Assuming he comes back. Or gets brought back, more likely."

"Josip seemed so sure," said Brenda. "That gave me a funny feeling." They all were standing in their own rooms' doorways.

"Speaking of funny feelings," Alec said, "I thought I'd ask if anyone would rather that I call them by—*you* know—their *actual* real name. I see no reason why we have to use the ones *they* gave us, all the time. Among ourselves, for instance."

"Huh," said Carrie. She seemed to think that idea over. "Speaking for myself, I guess I'd just as soon be 'Carrie' all the time I'm here. Stay, like, what's the word? Anominous?"

In fact, what she'd decided right away was that she didn't want this bunch of creeps to *ever* know her name. The last thing that she'd want, when they got out of there, would be to have them *calling* her, or, worse yet, camping on her doorstep.

"Anonymous," said Alec, pointedly.

Brenda nodded. "And me," she said, "I might as well continue being 'Brenda' to you-all. None of this seems real to me, so far. It's like I'm in a play, a character called Brenda."

"Elizabeth is fine," Elizabeth agreed. Brenda thought

that getting her own room had changed Elizabeth, made her more . . . self-confident. And less dependent, that'd mean, which certainly was fine with her.

"All right," said Alec, and he sounded cross. "I'll just go on with 'Alec,' then. I don't give a damn. If everybody prefers to keep their real identity a big state secret, fine. I sure can, too. It's perfectly all right with me. If you asked me to, I'd call you X and Y and Z."

In fact, he was surprised and hurt that no one took him up on his suggestion. He'd sort of thought that he'd . . . articulated something everybody felt: that they'd had something true and personal—some aspect of themselves— replaced by something false, a label. Now, he'd simply have to make the best of it, and go on being 'Alec' all the time. At least it was, he thought, a fairly *dashing* label. Maybe, over time, this Alec would be something, after all.

"I think I'll take a little nap," he snapped. He hoped that seemed decisive to the other three. Decisive and mature. He went into his much-the-biggest room and closed the door.

That was the sort of thing he did at home, a lot. Go in his room and close the door and sit around and, mostly, draw. He'd gotten A's in art, but no one was impressed by that; it was regarded as a minor course. He didn't seem to have important things to do. English was a major course, however. He thought if he got good at writing, that would be important. The only trouble was he couldn't think of any plots for novels.

The more he thought about it, the more he was quite sure his father'd sold him to the gypsies—he was one of those. Not because his father had to have whatever paltry sum the gypsies had agreed to pay, but just to plain get rid of him. So's not to have to *see* him, anymore.

six

THE NEXT DAY and the next one passed quite un-
eventfully, for everyone but Brenda; Alec used the word
peculiarly, while writing in the illustrated journal he decided to begin, the second day. He found it would be
possible to hide a lot of pages in the mirrored headboard of
his bed.

Not that anything "peculiar" happened; that was just his
point. *Nothing* really happened. People sat around. And that
seemed fine, with Josip and Marina.

One of them was always in the house. The other one went
"out," somewhere. When asked, specifically, by Carrie,
what he did when he went out, Josip winked and smiled and
placed a finger on his cheek beside his nose, and told her
"Gypsy business." At home, the King and Queen would
cook, and clean, play music (on a sort of wooden flute, or a
guitar, or the piano), write something in a notebook, and do
garden work. At least those were the things the kids ob-
served them doing. Kings and Queens seemed interchange-
able, in terms of what they did, all day.

◆   ◆   ◆

The first morning that the four woke up in Gypsyworld, they went downstairs together. Alec orchestrated that, knocking on the others' doors, when he had finished in the bathroom, making everybody wait till everyone was ready. They expected to find out what they were meant to do— what they were doing there—at breakfast time.

Good luck. They ate their breakfasts—fruit, hot cereal with milk, and milk to drink, and tea—and no one told them anything, except it looked like rain, but they could use it. When everybody'd finished, they all sat there at the table, waiting.

"Anyone want more of anything?" Marina asked.

She got three head shakes and a soft "No, thank you," from Elizabeth.

"Sometime later on today, I bring home a lot of clothes," the Queen went on. "Clean socks and underwear and shirts and pants—so on so forth. I'll put them in the hall, up-stairs; everybody help yourself, okay?"

Now there were four nods, and Alec mumbled, "Fine."

"And, yes, today," said Josip, "when it gets to be—oh, twelve o'clock, high noon, I show you what there is for lunch. And help you make it, if you don't know how. But come *tomorrow*"—and he held a finger up—"everybody have to get their own."

"Wow," said Carrie, and there was a silence after that. Elizabeth put up her hand. Marina laughed.

"Raising hand is good for school, I guess, but not for home," she said. "Here, you speak, I listen. That's a prom-ise. Vice versa too, okay?"

"What should I do *now*?" Elizabeth inquired.

"Anything your little heart desires," Josip said. "That right, Marina?" And she nodded. "Kids here on vacation now, from school, the same as you. You do just like they do, right?"

"Aha, but we don't *know*," said Alec, pouncing, "what they're doing." He had the hope that this might lead to something, lead to *learning* something. You could hear it in his voice, in that "Aha."

"Doing different jobs," said Josip. "Building character—aha!—and learning stuff about the world. Goofing off, I bet, and flirting with each other. All kinds of things! *You* know!"

"Goofing off and *flirting*?" Carrie said. "You're expecting us to just act *natural*?"

There was a pause. Josip and Marina looked at one another.

"Hoping so," she finally said. "Yes, really hoping so." He nodded his agreement.

◆　◆　◆

Brenda was the first to leave the grounds. Everybody'd hung around that morning. People made their beds, maybe out of desperation. There wasn't anything to do.

"You don't have TV?" Carrie asked Marina, meaning "all you gypsies."

"No," she said. "Not in this house, right now. Is on the *fritz*!" She laughed, mostly at the look on Carrie's face.

Alec asked the Gypsy Queen if he could take a book outside, one of the ones from in the living room, and she said sure. Brenda watched him choose a really boring-looking volume with dark blue binding, big and fat. Alec also asked Marina if she had some paper he could borrow—plain, unlined—plus a pencil or a pen. She told him where to find those things, and Carrie asked if he was going to write a letter home.

"I thought I'd maybe take a walk downtown, this afternoon," Brenda said to Carrie and Elizabeth, when Alec had gone out the door. "You want to come with me?"

She watched while Carrie thought that over. She was sure that Carrie'd *like* to go. Perhaps with someone. But maybe not with her.

"Nah, I thought I'd wash my hair," she finally said. "Seeing as it didn't rain." She didn't look at Brenda, saying that.

"How about Elizabeth?" said Brenda. "You want to take a walk? Maybe we could meet some gypsy kids." She was careful not to say "your age."

Elizabeth was not enthusiastic.

"No," she said. "No way."

"Why not?" Carrie said to her. "You 'fraid of gypsy kids? You 'fraid that they won't like you? That they'll think you're strange?"

"No," Elizabeth repeated. "I just don't want to go."

"Well, you don't have to," Brenda said. "I'll scout around, and tell you all about it, when I get back home. And maybe you'll decide to come *next* time."

" 'Home'?" said Carrie. "You're calling this place 'home'? Just because you think the gypsies want you to? You *are* a suck-butt, Brenda."

"Give me a break, all right?" said Brenda. She went upstairs and to her room, to read that cartoon book, again.

◆　◆　◆

As she meandered "downtown," after lunch, Brenda kept on wishing she was somewhere else, instead of Gypsyworld— assuming that she had to be away from home. She wished she was in France. France would have been much easier to deal with. France, she knew, *existed;* she could find it on a map. And it had the Eiffel Tower and Montparnasse and a street they called the Champs Elysées (*"Shawnz Elliezay,"* she thought), right there in Paris, or *"Pa-ree."* She'd heard that blacks and other colored people got on well, in France.

Gypsyworld, however, was an unknown quantity. It probably existed—she was *somewhere,* after all—but she did not know thing one about it. Who the people were, or what their attitudes might be, what language they would speak, or even names of any of their streets and buildings. She'd never seen a "Gypsyworld" on any map. She didn't have a famous ancestor that came from there; her mother would have mentioned it.

No (she thought), *Gypsyworld* she didn't know thing one about. She could barely swear it *was.* At this point, it was mostly hearsay.

But, nice-*looking* hearsay, no denying that. She'd decided that the neighborhood that she was walking through was middle class—not really rich, but far from poor. None of the homes she'd passed were, like, *estates*—outrageous as to size—but all of them were well kept up. And all their owners must have had green thumbs, because their yards were all, almost without exception, full of healthy, growing things: flowers, grapes on arbors, berry bushes, fruit trees, vegetables. Her mother'd talked about how, growing up, she'd helped out with her parents' garden, in the South. She always made it clear that doing that was something she'd been glad to see the last of. Brenda supposed it took some work to make a yard look . . . *lush,* like these all did. But going by the hammocks she saw strung between the trees, gypsies liked to put their feet up, too.

One impression that she'd gotten at the King and

Queen's was holding true: there wasn't lots of traffic on these streets. Although she saw another double-decker bus with lots of people on it, cars and trucks were rare, compared to home, and most of them were small, and some of them were almost silent, making just a sort of *buzzing* sound. What there was a goodly number of was bicycles—not so much the racing kind as more like mountain bikes, except with baskets, and some of them pulled little trailers, even.

The few cars that there were had funny-looking license plates (except for one from Connecticut). They weren't uniform at all, these local plates. They were square and round and oblong and triangular. All had colorful designs or images (flowers, houses, one fat pig) painted or imprinted on their surfaces, as well as letter-number combinations. Some of them appeared to be homemade, as if a kid had made them, even; others looked quite gorgeous.

Seeing them made Brenda think that possibly there *was* a place called "Gypsyworld." Those license plates seemed right for such a place; they were what she'd call *exotic,* that's for sure. They also made her smile. That one car probably belonged to really recent immigrants (like her), some gypsies from Connecticut.

For the first part of her trip, Brenda was the only person on the sidewalk, but when her street dead-ended at a larger avenue (on which she turned and walked), she found herself with lots of other people.

Her heart beat faster. Now she could be in a danger zone. Josip and Marina were all right (or even "nice"), but possibly they had to act like that, as Gypsy King and Queen. She didn't know how other gypsies would behave.

Well, at first they were a nice surprise. Not only were they cheerful looking (mostly younger kids with mothers and some older folks—pretty standard shapes and sizes), but also they seemed very . . . *cosmopolitan* (a fancy word for "cool" she'd learned). In general, the people were a lot more dark than blond, and she heard a lot of foreign languages (*mais certainement*) mixed in with English—often in one sentence.

But after two blocks on the avenue, she noticed something else about the people, something not so hot. No one seemed to look directly at her. That had never happened to her in her life, before.

Oh, from time to time, perhaps somebody's eye would catch an *edge* of her, but it would always slide away, as if there wasn't anything about her worth admiring, or even checking out. She began to feel almost *invisible*.

As soon as she thought that, she gave a little start. Josip and Marina'd proved already that they knew a thing or two about strange herbs and roots and spices. Making her invisible might be a breeze, for them. She thought back, and soon suspected . . . lunch.

She had had a sandwich and iced tea. The iced tea she had made herself, and it had just been simple, normal, regular iced tea. The sandwich was a real good possibility, however. She'd made it out of something from the icebox, something that she would have said was chicken spread—a mixture with a lot of different things in it, for sure. Looking at it, you could never tell what-all the Gypsy King or Queen had put in it. And of course the *active* (as they say) ingredient— it could have been invisible, itself. There'd been a book her parents had, called *Invisible Man,* by Ralph Ellison. Her mother'd said it was a *classic,* that she had to read it some-time. But she hadn't done that yet, she hadn't got around to it. She wasn't into reading all that much; there was enough she had to do for school. But now she wished she'd read that one. It might have given her some clues.

But clues or no clues, there was still this situation. Brenda decided that she'd have to do a *test*—find out if she was visible, or not, to all these people. She simply had to know. She'd stand in someone's way and speak; she'd ask some person something.

She looked ahead of her, to choose a target. Yes (she thought), *there* was a woman coming who'd be perfect. She was middle aged, a little on the heavy side, and wore a necklace made of wooden beads all carved and painted to resemble different fruits and vegetables. The owner of that necklace (Brenda thought) would be a *socializing* sort of person.

"Excuse me," she began. She'd stepped right in the woman's path. And she had the perfect question, ready on her tongue, "but is there anyplace nearby where I could get a newspaper?"

The things that made the question so ideal were, *one,* that anyone could answer it and, *two,* she'd really like to get a paper. A paper, she had realized, would tell her where she was and *when* it was, as well. She hadn't yet ruled out the possibility that she was in a "time warp" of some sort—that maybe all of them inside that Winnebago had been driven into, like, another *era.*

Well, if that was so (she quickly learned), it wasn't one where positive responses were the rule.

"No, no, no," the woman started muttering, as soon as Brenda got the question out. "No, no, no, no, no. I'm sorry."

And, not looking at the girl at all, she stepped around her and kept going down the street.

At least she stepped around me, Brenda thought. *I'm (clearly) not invisible.* And that was good. Another good thing was:

she didn't feel afraid. The *woman* had seemed more afraid than she was, although fear was not *exactly* what she looked like she was feeling. She thought that it was more like sorrow, mingled with disgust.

Brenda decided she'd confront a different kind of person.

That idea occurred to her because she saw a prospect. He was a young man sitting on a bench beside a bus stop sign. A young man nicely dressed and nicely blessed (with lookin'-handsome genes). She couldn't swear that he was African-American, but he was something with a hyphen in it, she was pretty sure. He also looked as if he was the kind—the *type*—of fine young man that she'd hung out with, back before this Josip-and-Marina business started. He looked warm, as well as cool.

She sat down on the selfsame bench that he was on and crossed one leg. She didn't sit right next to him, nor did she stay a mile away. It was clear, at least to her, that she was being friendly but still dignified, in no way cheap, or pushy. She didn't turn toward him, but spoke into the empty air in front of her.

"I think I need some help," she said. "I don't know what's going on, or even where I am, exactly. All I know is that I got here with four other kids I'd never seen before. Josip and Marina—who tell us they're the Gypsy King and Queen— they're the ones who brought us, in a Winnebago van. Can you—would you—tell me where I am, and what the date is, now? Would you help me, please, somehow?"

She hadn't planned to make a rhyme, and so she turned in his direction at the end of that, a small, self-conscious smile in place. Which meant she saw *him* turn to look at *her*. She saw the . . . well, *expression* on his face, and it was one of kindness, interest, caring.

But then he seemed to shake himself. He got up quickly,

muttering, "Here comes my bus." With that, he went and stood beside the curb, and raised his hand to signal the approaching double-decker.

Before she knew what she was doing, Brenda started crying—just like that. She supposed (much later on, when she'd got calm enough to start supposing, once again) the reason for her tears was that she felt so terribly *alone,* just then. She'd heard of people being lonely in a crowd, but up to then she'd never been that kind of person.

She put her face down in her hands, and so she never saw the young man, now aboard the bus, when he was looking through its wide rear window, looking back at her.

The gypsies on the street kept walking by the bench, ignoring her completely. They just dealt with one another.

After a few minutes, Brenda pulled herself together, and stood up, and started walking "home."

seven

AFTER WHAT HAD HAPPENED to her on her way downtown, Brenda wasn't anything but glad to see the blue and white *maison* of Josip and Marina. Perhaps it wasn't *home* home, but at least it was familiar, and a place where people didn't jump on buses at the sight of her.

She saw a bike there on the rack outside the big front door, but she couldn't tell if it was Josip's or Marina's. Their bikes looked totally the same. But when she heard the music coming from the open window of the living room, she knew the Queen was home. She was the good piano player; Josip, he more fooled around. At the moment she was playing something powerful, full of flowing chords and kind of sad. Brenda walked across the lawn and sat down with her back against a tree.

Right away, she started to relax. One thing that she liked about this place: it didn't have a lot of bad smells in the air. To the contrary, in fact, Gypsyworld smelled *good*. Not in the same way a *cologne* smells good, or french fries when you're hungry; it didn't smell *of* anything, exactly. She thought that maybe what it smelled like was just air, pure air, before it's changed by all the million smells (some good, some bad) that *people* add to it. Brenda curled her toes and reached to touch them; then she settled back again and *really* felt relaxed. She liked lots of different kinds of music—rap or rock or R&B or moody stuff like she was hearing then— almost any music was a treat. Listening, she soon forgot how bothered she had been, downtown.

She'd never been the sort who moped and brooded. Once was bad enough, she always said. She didn't see the sense in going over rotten things that happened, time and time again, like certain people did.

For instance, how she did in school. It always was a disappointment to her parents—the grades she got, in school. But she disliked those C's and D's as much as they did. She'd have given anything to be the sort who knocked back books as easily as diet sodas in the summertime. But she wasn't/didn't/couldn't, and there wasn't any point in going on about it, in the way her parents did.

"At least I get along real good!" she'd yell at them, in desperation, when they really started to bear down on her, and throw mean words around, like "lazy," "worthless," "no account." They never gave her any credit for the things she did real well; they weren't easy, either. Trouble was, you didn't get a grade for understanding people, having friends.

"You think your looks and personality are all you need for college?" they'd then ask. "You think somebody's going to hire you for any kind of *decent* job because you got a pretty face and frisky-lookin' bottom?"

And she would shake her head, and cry, and try, and actually get by, but never do that great. And "great" was ". . . how you damn well *better* do, if you are black as well as female," as her father liked to say.

Luckily, she *did* get on real well with almost all the other kids in school, and teachers too, in fact. White or black, it didn't seem to make a difference. And it wasn't just because of how she looked, although of course that never hurt. What she noticed was: once she got to know a person some, she seemed to understand them pretty well. What she could do was put herself in someone else's place and sort of feel what they were feeling. What made them scared and mad, or tingle with delight. And once she knew those things, she'd act accordingly. Unlike a lot of other kids, she didn't feel the need to tease and bait, to be in people's faces all the time.

Sitting on the lawn outside that two-toned house, she was thinking that at least she liked the Gypsy King and Queen, and that the other kids were not that bad, though strange (and, in Carrie's case, right up there on the edge of hostile). And then, eventually, she started in debating in her mind if she should tell the King and Queen about what happened to her on her way downtown. It was possible that one of them could tell her why that woman and that boy had acted like they did. But would they? She could not be sure. Sometimes (she'd found this out at home) the best thing she could do was just not mention things—bad things—that happened anywhere away from home. The less "they" knew, the better, when it came to certain negative material. Smart girls kept their mouths shut.

Just then, the piece Marina had been playing came to a conclusion. Brenda waited for a minute to be sure that she was finished playing and, when no more music floated out the window, she got up and went inside.

But when she walked into the living room, the only person there was Carrie, sitting on the sofa with a towel around her head and staring into space.

"Hi," said Brenda. "I see you washed your hair all right."

"Mmm. Yeah, finally," Carrie said. She seemed a little out of it. Slowly, she unwound the turban from her head and started fluffing out her hair. "I ought to sit outside and let it dry, I guess."

"Where'd Marina go? I want to ask her something," Brenda said.

"Marina? I don't know. She went out someplace when I was getting in the shower. Josip's back there in the kitchen," Carrie said. "He's making dinner. Chopped something— bat's meat, maybe—in tomato sauce. With toadstools." She wrinkled up her nose. "D'you suppose that means it's Wednesday?"

Brenda smiled. "Marina's out?" she said. "So, who was playing the piano?"

"Me," said Carrie. "If you mean just now. I just finished playing something."

"*Really?*" Brenda said. "No, wait. You trying to kid me?" Carrie shook her head. "My God, you're really *good*!"

Carrie shook her head again, and made that little get-lost gesture with her hand.

"Thanks. But, well, it's just a thing I do," she said. "It's no big deal. A lot of people play. Doin' it won't pay the rent, as my mom says. Or get me into college, either. You know school. If you don't do great in math and English . . ." She did that little wave again and Brenda nodded. "So, how was downtown, anyway?"

"I don't know. I didn't get there," Brenda said. She hesitated. Carrie'd never been this friendly. She wondered if the music was responsible. Maybe playing it had made her sort of sad—and humble. More *available*. It also was the first time that they'd been alone together, just the two of them.

"It turned out to be too far," she added. "So I came on back."

"I figured you were going to get Elizabeth a birthday present," Carrie said. "It's tomorrow, right? Her birthday?"

"Oh, gosh," said Brenda. "I forgot. That's awful."

Carrie shrugged. "I doubt she'll be expecting stuff from us," she said. "It's not like we're best friends with her, or anything. And besides, how could we? Who's got any gypsy money? I only had a half a dollar in my pocket when they grabbed me. Or *procured* me, or whatever happened." Her voice had gotten hard, again. "Stolen, bought—what difference does it make?"

"Yeah," said Brenda. All of a sudden she was overtaken by an urge to . . . well, *confide* in Carrie, tell her something personal and true. She wanted to feel close to someone, her, another girl. It seemed to her that this'd be the time for that, assuming there was ever going to be one.

"I wouldn't be at all surprised," she said, "if I was one of them the gypsies *bought*. What I was thinking was: say my parents were convinced the gypsies weren't pimps or murderers . . ." And Carrie smirked. "I could see them working out a deal and getting rid of me. I haven't made them too damn proud, so far. If anything, the opposite." She made a rueful face.

"Tell me about it," Carrie said. "My parents—well, the stuff I said before about my mother was a crock. She hasn't called me any lovey-dovey name for years. All we do is fight, my mother and myself. She's always saying I'm a tramp— like *she* should talk—and telling me she's going to throw me out. My stepfather's a creep. He lives off her and sneaks around and tries to get his hands on me—*you* know—but I won't let him. The both of them would sell me in a minute, cheap. You kidding?" She stood up and rubbed the towel against her head some more.

"I guess the fact is all of us could *possibly* be stolen goods," said Brenda, softly. "But all of us could just as easily be paid for, too—on sale. I'm thinking that it's good that we don't know which one we are. This way, we can all think anything we want." She paused. "We can think good things about each other, if we want to, even about that little rooster, Dennis."

Carrie didn't look at her.

"I'm going outside, now," she said.

◆　◆　◆

Once out there in the yard, Carrie thought she'd go and look at Josip and Marina's garden, just as a thing to do. She'd never been the kind to have plants in her room, that sort of thing. But she'd also never been in any place like Gypsy-world, where people *had* a garden. She sort of wished she hadn't said what she had said to Brenda—that stuff about her mother and herself, her stepfather. She wondered why she had. It must have been because she'd been thrown off by Brenda being all that nice and . . . regular, herself. It was about the first time she had had a conversation with a black girl since she'd grown up, matured. Probably the only reason she'd had it was there wasn't anyone she knew around. And the gypsies, obviously, did not have any . . . attitudes.

She saw that geeky Alec was right there, beside the garden, sitting on the grass. He had a piece of paper lying on the big old book he'd borrowed from the Queen, and he was writing on it. Or—no, wait, he wasn't writing, he was drawing something, she was pretty sure. But when he saw her coming, he snatched the paper up and stuck it in the book. He had a bunch of other sheets in there already.

She broke the ice: "Hey, Alec." What the hell, there wasn't anyone around.

"Hi, Carrie," he replied. "You washed your hair, I see." He picked up something off the grass.

I'm living with a bunch of Sherlock Holmeses, Carrie thought. "Yup," she said. And, "Hey, what's that you've got? Is that a *feather*? Hey, it's beautiful."

"Yeah," he said. "I found it over there." He pointed toward the property next door. "The neighbors must have peacocks—or *a* peacock. It's a peacock feather."

"Wow," said Carrie. "Can I see?" He handed it to her. She looked at the amazing colors in the thing, the changing colors in its eye. It was pretty clear he wasn't going to let her keep the feather. What if she just took it?

"Nice find," she said. She gave it back to him.

"Yeah," said Alec, once again. "Maybe there's another one, over there, somewhere. I just saw this one, but, well, I didn't really look for any more."

"I'll check," she said, and wandered off, away from him. She thought that Alec was a funny-looking kid, the sort of nerdy grind she'd never had a thing to do with, home. And here in Gypsyworld, she'd just walked up to him and had a little conversation.

First, a black girl, and then a geek. Two for two. She touched her face and wondered if she'd broken out in spots. She had to hope this wasn't like that TV show. There'd better not be hidden cameras around.

◆ ◆ ◆

It *was* spaghetti that they had for dinner. And everybody seemed to like the sauce that Josip made. It certainly was different. Brenda whispered, just to Carrie, that she couldn't taste the bat's meat or the toadstools, either. Carrie laughed and everybody else looked puzzled, or surprised.

"So—tomorrow we got birthday girl," the King said, tearing up a piece of "locally Italian bread," as he described it. He was beaming at Elizabeth. "Entering her teens— *fantastic!*"

Elizabeth looked down and shook her head. "It's no big deal," she muttered.

"Incorrect!" cried Josip. "This is great big deal, in Gypsyworld. Why not?"

"Yes," Marina said. "You see, Elizabeth, thirteen is most important age with us. Like Jewish people, in a way, but different. Not religious."

"Thirteen is an *important* age? You're kidding," Carrie said. She couldn't help herself. *Kids* looked forward to becoming teens, but that was it. To adults, teens were just important pains.

Josip had that finger up, again. But he was smiling broadly, too. One thing Carrie had to give him credit for: even when he said a thing he really wanted you to listen to, he didn't act all powerful, and make a big deal of *himself*. He didn't seem at all conceited for a king, she thought— although of course she hadn't met a lot of other ones she could compare him to.

"In Gypsyworld, a person has the right to speak in public meetings and to vote for public officers, at thirteen years," Josip said. "Including King and Queen." He laughed. "It's only one to twelves who get to say, 'Hey, don't blame *me* for Josip and Marina.'" And he laughed some more.

"Of course we gypsies listen up to all opinions," said Marina. "One to twelves included, in the home. Everyone has point of view, and jobs to do, and needs to be considered. But, tell you something: kids, they not in charge of Gypsyworld. Not to please misunderstand me. Some things take experience and practice—lotsa them, in fact. Other things a person has to study hard, and long, before they know. But every point of view has preciousness, with us. An' you know why?"

" 'Cause gypsies know that every *one* is precious," Josip answered. He didn't notice Brenda look at Carrie, smile at her. He'd kept his royal finger up. "Even ones I don' agree with, or can't understand. How can I look clearly through the eyes of someone from Rwanda, or Tibet?" He had to laugh again. "Even ones who can't stand my spaghetti sauce—I call them 'precious,' too." He dropped his finger down. "End of precious conversation."

"But suppose somebody—me, for instance—wanted to continue . . . shall we say, *conversing?* On that subject?" That was Alec. Sure, who else? thought Brenda. He pushed his glasses up his nose. His eyes were gleaming. With obnoxiousness, thought Carrie.

"Hey, go ahead!" cried Josip. "Fine with me. What *I* said—end of *my* part of that conversation. *I* said all that I could think of. But everybody *else* can say till cows come home. Why not?"

"Well, suppose *I* said I think your theory's crazy?" Alec said. "Hitler wasn't precious. Lots of people aren't."

"Person *always* precious," said Marina. "*Activity*—what someone does—is different story. Gypsy children not to act like brats. Mosquito comes to bite me, it gets squash. Stealing, lying, killing not allowed."

"So, basically, the *outcome* is the same all over," Alec said. "People who have power make the rules about activity. And anyone who goes against those rules gets squashed. Thirteen-year-olds included. This 'precious' business seems to be a question of semantics." Alec looked around the table. He wasn't one hundred percent certain what *semantics* meant, but he'd heard his father use the term a lot, sometimes to shut his mother up.

"No, is not semantics—something else," the Queen replied. "*You'll* see."

"Well, if I see people acting any differently toward teenage kids in Gypsyworld, I'll be amazed, I'll tell you that much," Alec said. "As far as I'm concerned, putting people down is simple, basic human nature."

Marina had gotten up and started to collect the plates. Elizabeth stood up, as well.

"I'm going to wash the dishes," she announced. "It's my last day as a kid. Then, tomorrow, I can vote for someone else to do them: Prince of Dishes." She looked at Alec and she smiled a little smile. "Maybe I'll start putting people down, myself."

Everybody, even Alec—even Carrie—just cracked up.

♦　♦　♦

When Brenda got upstairs, that night, she went to bed but couldn't sleep. There seemed to be so much to think about. And, in addition, there were voices, people talking at the dinner table, almost underneath her room. Two of them were Josip and Marina, but there were two other voices, also—two strange and different *tones* of voice down there, both masculine.

Brenda slid out of her bed. "Miss Nosy Parker," as her

mother sometimes said. She remembered that there was a grill set into her bedroom floor, a sort of hot-air register, the kind of thing that you could close and open to allow warm air from underneath the room to rise up through the floor and into it, or not. In this case, warm air from the kitchen. Moving noiselessly, she reached the grill and knelt beside it. The thing was closed; she thumbed it open and the voices, although muffled still, got clearer. She could almost hear what they were saying, *almost* understand.

The trouble was . . . they weren't speaking English. "Jimble-jamble-jumble," one would say, and someone else would answer (though at greater length), "Bay-badoo-badah."

Then, suddenly, *"Ce n'est pas vrai."* They all were speaking French! "That isn't so," a stranger man had said.

His voice continued, going much too fast for Brenda, totally incomprehensible. And angry. But ending with, much slower, *"Ils sont les enfants terribles, gâtés, perdus."* Brenda was pretty sure she got those words all right, all but one of them: "They are children terrible (something), lost." (It was just as well she didn't know what *gâtés* meant. It's "spoiled.")

The Queen's voice, answering, was softer, so much softer, Brenda couldn't catch a word. And then the King got his two francs' worth in, also very gently, almost pleadingly.

Another rapid-fire comment, from the other man this time, starting, *"Nous verrons . . ."* ("We shall see") and impossible to follow till the end. *"Au revoir,"* said almost everyone. Footsteps, and a door closed.

Brenda got up off the floor and went and sat. There was a guest-room-type wing chair beside the window, and she sat there, looking out. It wasn't quite full moon, but she could recognize the shapes of trees and bushes on the big back lawn. She watched a cat go fast across the open space.

She tried to understand the fragment of the conversation that she'd heard. Two men she didn't know had sounded angry, speaking to the King and Queen; Josip and Marina had been trying to calm them down and reassure them. Was she being paranoid to think that maybe those two angry men were mad about *their* being there, in Gypsyworld? Were she and those four other kids the "children terrible, and something else, and lost"? It certainly seemed possible.

She began to wonder why she hadn't told about her trip downtown at dinner. She could have brought it up while they were eating, and that way everybody would have heard whatever explanation Josip and Marina gave. They might have *had to* give one, really. If they were saying gypsies thought that everyone was precious, how would they account for all the meanness she'd encountered? She hadn't been so precious to the young man and that lady with the funny necklace, clearly. And to those two that had been down there in the kitchen, she might be even worse than that: "terrible" and "lost."

Against her better judgment, knowing things were always much more scary in the dark, Brenda started thinking real depressing thoughts about her present situation. Was there a chance (she asked herself) that she was there in Gypsyworld for good? That she would never see her friends again, her parents, everything familiar she'd grown up with? She'd been assuming they'd go back—be taken back—in . . . probably some kind of "little while." But now she wondered if that was a false assumption, even a ridiculous assumption.

It sure would be the pits (thought Brenda) if she had to

stay in Gypsyworld for all her life and only Josip and Marina and those four strange kids would even *talk* to her. How would she . . . get *married,* have a family? Even if the King was able to *perform* a wedding, Alec and that Dennis—assuming he came back, as Josip said he would—were *unthinkable* as . . . well, prospective husbands. She would end up as a sad old maid!

That thought—that possibility—brought her to the edge of tears, again. Probably she would have cried (self-pity is a most contemptible, but powerful emotion), if she hadn't seen another moving shadow down on the lawn. Far bigger than a cat, it also came across the open space at speed, but this one stopped at the back door. It was a person, someone.

Brenda thought she heard a knock. She must have, for the back door opened suddenly, and light streamed out of it. To her amazement, standing in that brightness was the young man she had seen downtown, the one whom she had talked to, by the bus stop.

She blinked, and he had disappeared; the door had shut. She'd heard it close behind him.

For some ten minutes after that, Brenda teased herself with the suggestion that she march downstairs, confront the King and Queen (and him!), demand to know exactly what was going on.

But all along, she knew she wasn't going to do that. Sometimes, she thought, the less you seem to know, the better. Smart girls kept their mouths shut.

She crept back into bed.

eight

❧

ON THE MORNING that Elizabeth became thirteen, Alec was awake at 6 a.m. He'd decided it was up to him to make the day as memorable as possible for her; it was his responsibility. After all, he *was* "the oldest one." He welcomed being that. It was something meaningful, a special thing about him, almost like an office or a title, such as President, Director, *Elder*.

Elizabeth, however, was the baby of the family, "the youngest one." And—he might as well admit it—she was, in fact, his favorite member of the group. Brenda was all right—good enough to serve as second-in-command—but she was independent and good looking, not the sort of person who'd warm up to him, he didn't think. He imagined she'd gone out with older men, at home. And Carrie and the absent Dennis were a pair of wise guys, people with no sense of values, of the proper way of doing things—though Carrie *might* be shaping up a little. Elizabeth, however, seemed to understand. Alec thought she was far wiser than her years. She just *looked* quite young. But as the King had pointed out, she wasn't any *child*, not anymore.

At seven o'clock, Alec started knocking, softly but insistently, on Brenda's door. And then, when he heard movement in her room, on Carrie's. Soon, both girls were peering out their partly opened doors, and looking at him very crossly.

"Hi, good morning," Alec said. "I know it's early, but—I thought perhaps the three of us should wake Elizabeth together. Be the first to wish her happy birthday." Alec giggled. "Maybe give her thirteen swats and one to grow on."

Carrie looked at him as if he'd said they ought to leave the house and run out on the lawn and do a dance in honor of all toadstools. Brenda just compressed her lips and shook her head.

"No way," she said. "That's crazy. We go busting in her room like that, she'd have a fit, I bet. I know *I* would. And she's too old for getting spanked." Brenda wasn't asking, she was telling.

"But don't you think," said Alec, pitching his appeal primarily at her, "she really would appreciate the thought of us . . . well, making, like, a little *fuss* for her, first thing?"

Brenda thought that over. "*Possibly* she would," she finally said. "You're right. Maybe we could sing." She looked at Carrie. "How about it? You could do it, couldn't you? Make us sound a little special?"

"What?" said Carrie. "Singing 'Happy Birthday'? *Jesus,* Brenda. You're as bad as he is." She looked as if she might be just about to close her door.

But Brenda came out in the hall and faced her. She clasped her hands together, almost dropping to one knee.

"*Please,*" she pleaded. She was overdoing, making fun. "Carrie, please—a little harmony, all right? *One* time? I *know* that you can do it, and we'll never ask again." She had on sweatpants and a big gray baggy cotton T.

Carrie had to smile. "All *right,* already. But only if the two of you can stay in tune. And take it slow, all right?" She came out in the hall. She was in her underwear, a camisole and black bikini briefs. She crossed her arms and cleared her throat. "Anytime you're ready."

Brenda started it. She knew she had an okay voice, herself, and she hit it with a nice slow bluesy beat: "Ha-ppy birth-day to you . . ."

Alec joined her on the next phrase and, to her surprise, he also sang in tune—a little geekily, but right there on the notes. And when Carrie jumped in on the "Happy birthday, dear Eliza-*beth,*" Brenda's eyes went wide with both surprise and happiness. It sounded *great!* They stretched the last line to the max.

As soon as it had ended, both girls jumped back into their rooms and closed their doors. Alec stood there in the middle of the hall alone, the picture of uncertainty. But then he nodded, suddenly, and did the same as they had done.

♦ ♦ ♦

Alec liked to feel the effort they had made, that he had *organized,* had set a perfect tone for that important day. Elizabeth, both soothed and warmed by such a vocal tribute (this was Alec's explanation, anyway), was the last one down to breakfast. Everybody shouted "Happy birthday!" and they stood and clapped when she came in the kitchen; the King and Queen, together, went and wrapped her up in one huge hug, while planting noisy kisses on both cheeks. Brenda followed suit, without a moment's hesitation, and then Carrie, swept into the spirit of the thing, did also. Alec, wearing one of his most geeky grins, kept standing at his place, but turned to face Elizabeth. And, when Carrie stepped away from her, Elizabeth faced *him,* as well. For just a moment they were frozen, she (perhaps) by expectation, he by awkwardness, confusion. But finally he found, at least, his voice.

"Happy thirteenth!" he boomed, and *then* he moved, stumble-stepping forward with his hand outstretched. She took it, smiling shyly, happily, and pumped it up and down.

"Thank you, Alec," she said softly, letting go.

◆　◆　◆

That morning, all four kids—Elizabeth included—did some decorating in the dining area, using stuff Marina had: crepe paper, and balloons, and even place cards. Alec, having asked the Queen for colored paper, scissors, thread, and wire hangers, created a huge HAPPY BIRTHDAY mobile, which he hung like an enormous lettered chandelier, right over the middle of the table. Even Carrie was impressed by that, how quick and confident he was while making up the mobile, and then how *good* it looked when he was done. Like modern art, she thought.

While they were together, Alec mentioned that he thought he might go downtown, later on.

"You went yesterday?" he said to Brenda. "Carrie said you had."

"Not exactly," Brenda said. "I started out." She had the feeling that Marina, doing something in the kitchen near the stove, had stopped to listen.

"It was farther than I thought," she said. "So I came back." The Queen resumed activity.

"Well, if there's time, I'd like to go," said Alec. He called over to the Queen. "Marina! Is there time for me to go downtown and back this afternoon? Before the birthday dinner? I don't suppose you'd let me use a bicycle . . . ?"

Marina turned around. "I would," she said, "except the gears on mine are busted. We both been using Josip's. I suppose you *could* walk down and back in time, but it's a hike."

She did a shrug that even Brenda could admire, and then turned away, again. She hadn't looked at Brenda, Brenda noticed. "Maybe you should wait a day or two," came floating, as an afterthought, from where the Queen was standing, by the stove.

"I don't know," said Alec. "I could use the exercise." That made Carrie stop the napkin folding she was doing, but before she could come up with just the perfect cut, he kept on talking.

"You want to take another whack at getting there?" he said to Brenda. "And how about *you*, Carrie?"

Brenda shook her head. "No, thanks," she said. "I told the Queen I'm going to help her with a secret project, here. *Top* secret, highly classified. The kitchen, by the way, will be off bounds to everyone who hasn't gotten clearance from security—in other words, the rest of you." She thought that maybe she should warn him, but then she had another idea cross her mind: Suppose that it was only me—just *me* the gypsies didn't want to talk to?

"Me, I've got to paint my toenails," Carrie said. "And if you're interested, Miss *Brenda,* even if you *paid* me I would never hang around in any kitchen full of baking smells, with frosting bowls to lick, and—oops!" She covered up her mouth and bugged her eyes.

"Gee, I'm sorry, there, Elizabeth," she added moments later. "I hope I didn't spoil their big *surprise.*"

But Elizabeth just laughed, held up a finger, and produced a not-bad imitation of a standard Carrie gesture, the Get-Outa-Here. Carrie had to laugh at that, herself.

"I guess I'll go, then," Alec said. He didn't sound as if he wanted to. "*Someone* ought to, and it looks like I'm elected."

"That's up to you," said Brenda. "I don't see the 'ought to' in it. If I were you, I'd wait, just like Marina said."

Alec looked at her suspiciously. Her attitude—*their* attitude—had made him feel two ways at once: suspicious and uncertain. Those, he realized, were most—perhaps *the* most—familiar feelings in his life, so far. If you didn't count *out of it,* and *awkward.*

"I'll probably go anyway," he said.

♦ ♦ ♦

As they had planned, Brenda and Marina made the birthday cake that afternoon. Brenda'd never made a cake from scratch, before.

"It's just as if you're making up a cake mix, right?" she asked the Queen, as they got started. "Why don't you save a lot of time and effort? Let somebody do it for you? *Buy* a box of mix?"

"Is better this way," said Marina. "I take responsibility, you see? I like to know what's in my cake." She paused and added, "In my everything, I guess."

While they were working in the kitchen, Carrie didn't do her toenails, after all. Instead, she spent some time at the piano in the living room. Elizabeth lay on the floor in there and listened.

"Don't you think she's *good?*" said Brenda to the Queen.

"Oh, yes," Marina said. "You bet. Is possibly her big intelligence."

"Intelligence?" said Brenda. She was creaming butter for the frosting, working hard at it. "Oh. But you mean *talent.*"

"Sure," Marina said. "Same thing. Like Alec says, 'a question of semantics.' All talents are intelligence, and vice versa. Many different kinds of both. Each one useful in a different way. Why not?"

"Wait," said Brenda. She set down the mixing bowl. "Like, back home we have those IQ tests and SATs. You know what they are?" And Marina nodded. "What you get on *them* determines if you're smart—intelligent—or not. Them and your grades in school. You know that's true, correct?"

"Is true 'back home,' " Marina said. "Not here in Gypsy-world. We say different situations call for different smarts. High-IQ-type smarts extremely useful, sometimes. Sure. But not in others. No great use in making birthday cake, for instance. More examples: You may be much smarter than myself in looking for the cause of cancer. But *I* may be much smarter when a hungry lion's chasing us. You understand? Different kind of talent gets involved."

This was a whole new way of looking at the world, to Brenda. It seemed to do away with certain negatives, all right—"dumb jock," for instance.

"Yes, I see that," she said. "But how about prestige, importance, status? Do runners get the same respect as doctors, here?"

"Maybe not quite," said the Queen. "Fairness never easy to arrange. But, yes, I say we getting there. It helps when people see the point."

"Oh, sure," said Brenda, and she waved a hand, but cheerfully. "That's the way you wiggle out of everything. Bring up your old *point,* again."

"Yes, *please*," Marina said. "And now, you got that butter creamed? We gonna add the sugar and vanilla . . ."

"Just one last thing," said Brenda, reaching for the bowl. "Suppose a person's good at . . . making friends, let's say. *Avoiding* making enemies. Would he—the person—be considered smart, *intelligent,* in Gypsyworld?"

"Of course," Marina said. "Why not? Is most important talent, needed very much, all times, all places." She lifted up her head and listened to the music coming from the living room. "Music making too, you see?"

◆　◆　◆

The birthday cake was finished, frosted, sitting on the counter, and the chicken was already roasting in the red clay pot, when Alec made it back from "downtown." Brenda, from the living room, heard him tromping up the stairs, and go into his room, and close the door.

She wasn't sure what to deduce from that behavior. It might be that he'd bought Elizabeth a present and was stowing it away up there, till later. But it also *could* mean that he'd found the atmosphere downtown as strange and threatening as she had—and that he was upset. If his trip had been a big success, she was pretty sure it wouldn't be too long before she heard about it. Alec looked to be the kind who'd do a little crowing.

But that never happened. He didn't come downstairs until Marina called him, and the food was on the table. The Queen had ruled they'd have a "U.S. Sunday dinner" for the birthday celebration: roast chicken with gravy, mashed potatoes and peas, ice cream and cake. She'd said to Brenda and to Carrie that in Gypsyworld they ate a lot of fish (which many people raised themselves, in backyard pools and tanks, and which had been in the spaghetti sauce, the night before), lesser amounts of chicken, and "a ton of beans and rice"—she smacked her lips—"in different sauces." Neither of the girls had seen a red clay pot, before, and Brenda'd only heard of people using pressure cookers, which the Queen had said were superfast, and healthy. Carrie was pleased to notice that the royal kitchen held a microwave, which was the one appliance she had used back home—in addition to her hair dryer.

As everyone filed in the dining room to take their seats, Josip put two little boxes tied with fat red ribbon on the table, at the head of it. And then he pulled that chair out, *his* chair, for Elizabeth.

"These presents are from all of Gypsyworld," he said, "including everybody here. So you remember it, and us, for always."

Just at that moment, Alec hurried in the room. In his hand he had what looked to be a big long envelope, quite flat. It seemed to be homemade, of sheets of unlined paper, glued or taped together. On one side of it, it said ELIZA-BETH, in huge inked letters, like the ones you see beginning Middle Ages manuscripts, the kind the monks would make. He heard what Josip said, as he came in.

"And here's one other silly thing," he told Elizabeth, and put it by her place. He looked flustered, at a loss for words.

"It really isn't anything," he added, "but we thought you ought to have it. Some of us"—he looked around the table—"well, it made us think of you."

And with that, and after two long strides, he sat down in his chair and gulped some water from his glass.

"Yeah," said Carrie, "it's a rubber glove for doing dishes with, and if you're really good, you'll get the other one when you're *four*teen."

"So, let's eat first and open presents after," Josip said. "No need for rubber gloves till at the end, not so? And anyway, I'm starving for some birthday dinner."

But then he clapped his forehead with an open palm. "Figs!" he cried. "I am forgetting birthday wine!"

He leaped to his feet and disappeared in the direction of his bedroom. Moments later, he was back, a dark green bottle swinging in his hand. He pulled the cork; Marina fetched some glasses, ruby red up top, clear as crystal stemmed below, and Josip went around the table, pouring.

"Toast!" he said, "to our sweetheart of the day, Elizabeth." And all the other people raised their glasses to the little girl and sipped, Alec looking borderline ecstatic.

But just as Josip sat back down, there was the sound of knocking on the big front door.

"Lots of Lords!" cried Josip. "Will I *never* eat?" He went to answer it.

The King was gone a little while—Marina started passing food around—and they could hear the rumble of his voice, conversing with another man. When, finally, the front door closed again, they heard some footsteps, coming back.

Two sets of footsteps.

"Am I the prophet?" Josip said. "Or what? Look! Is *Dennis,* coming *home*!" He had the boy in front of him, more or less propelling him along. Dennis wasn't looking overjoyed.

"Son of a *gun,*" said Carrie. She looked amused, excited, maybe even pleased. The other kids were more laid back— and also speechless. Alec and Brenda had the same short set of thoughts: Things were sort of shaking down at Josip and Marina's, everyone was getting on okay. They'd only seen Dennis in the Winnebago, and he'd seemed impetuous, a little hard to get along with. They wondered how he'd blend in, now. Elizabeth was mostly fearful for her party.

Marina went to get the boy a plate, a glass, a napkin, and utensils. Carrie moved her things to make a place for him between herself and Brenda.

Josip said, his finger up, "I know that everybody curious concerning Dennis, but now is not the time for him to hold the floor. For now, is birthday party going on. Elizabeth is turn thirteen today," he said to Dennis, finger down, "as you perhaps remember. So *that's* what we are celebrate, with wine and chitter chatter, yes? Why not? Later, when you all upstairs, Dennis tell you anything he wants to."

And that was how it went. Josip and Marina started up the "chitter chatter," but the others soon joined in, except for Dennis. People tried to draw him out, but his replies and comments were all muted: "Oh?" and "Yes, I see," and "Gravy, please," and "Thank you." He ate a lot of everything.

After ice cream and the chocolate cake were served and eaten, Elizabeth was urged to open up her presents.

Brenda thought she did it *great*—this opening-of-presents deal. She made it, like, a ceremony, picking up each present, holding it in front of her on both flat palms, and smiling down on it. She seemed to weigh, admire, think about the package first, before she very slowly opened it. She started with the little boxes, the ones the King had put down by her place.

The first one held a carving of a fish, made out of wood. It was extraordinary work, completely lifelike, small and delicate, and painted vivid colors. Her eyes got huge, her mouth became a perfect little O, the moment that she took the lid off the box and saw the present, lying on its bed of cotton.

She picked it up, but gently, carefully, and held it out so everyone could see it.

"Thank you, everyone," she said. "Our friend, the fish. How excellent; I love it." And she clasped it to her heart.

The second box contained a necklace made of shiny, polished stones: six green ones, then a black, six green ones, then a black—four sets of those.

"Oh," she said. "So beautiful. I've never had a thing this beautiful to wear."

She held the necklace up, then put it carefully around her neck. From looking at her, Brenda knew that she was *feeling* beautiful, right then.

That left the envelope. She picked it up and stared down at the lettering; she pronounced her name: "E-liz-a-beth." Then she opened up the envelope and slid out what was in there. It was not a rubber glove; it was a peacock feather.

"Wow!" Elizabeth exclaimed. She held it high in front of her. "What is it?"

"It's a peacock feather, silly," Carrie said.

And, as other exclamations came from other people at the table, Carrie switched her eyes from the feather to Alec. *He* was looking at Elizabeth and, the odd thing was, he was looking much less geeky than she'd ever seen him.

nine

⬦

THEY ASSEMBLED up in Alec's room.

"Let's go in yours, it's much the biggest," Carrie said to him, while going up the stairs. And then, remembering, she added, "Hey—of course! It's his room, too. You get to sleep with *Alec,* Dennis!" Her eyes were sparkling. She could only see the back of Alec's head, but she could turn to look at Dennis.

Dennis curled a lip at her. (OH, SURE, he thought.) But it wasn't an unfriendly curl, she thought.

Brenda didn't like all these developments. What did they call it on the evening news? A *late-breaking story?* "Reporters had a hard time keeping up with what went on in Gypsyworld today . . ." She watched the happenings inside the room. Alec, who'd hurried to be first one through the door, flopped down on the unmade bed, the big one with the mirrored headboard. Dennis looked around and chose an armchair; then he pushed the table next to it around in front of him, so he could put his feet on it. Carrie took the other armchair, close to him. That left the little fold-out couch unoccupied, so Brenda and Elizabeth sat down on it, together, like a couple of twins. It felt funny, doing that, and so they smiled at one another.

For about a count of five, nobody spoke.

Then, *"So,"* said Alec, and then not so loudly, "how come you came back? Did someone bring you? I thought I heard another voice out there."

"Yeah"—Dennis didn't look at him—"the *cops,*" he said. (The IDIOTS, he thought, they look as if they've made themselves at home. What were their STUPID names? Alec, and *Elizabeth*—he'd picked that up again at dinner. And the cute one, she was . . . *Carey,* was it? Some DAMN thing like that.)

"It was the *second* time they'd picked me up," he said. "I tried to hitch a ride from them, the first time. Nobody else would stop. I tried to tell them what was going down—but they said I oughta go on back to Josip and Marina's."

"Wait," said Carrie. She leaned forward in her chair, her elbows on her thighs, hands clasped together on her knees. "Start at the beginning. When you left the van . . . that was, what? three days ago? What did you do first?"

"I flat out headed for the hills," he said. (Like, ZOOM!) "I wanted to get out of town, and so I walked and walked and walked, and all the time that I was walking, I was also trying to hitch a ride. An' people would slow down, but when they got a real good look at me, they'd jump back on the gas again, and keep on going. I felt like I had *lepersy,* or something."

"That's really *interesting,*" said Alec. "Earlier today, *I* started walking *down*town, and as soon as I got to that big main avenue . . ." He twisted on the bed and pointed out a window, vaguely.

"Alec," Carrie said. "You *mind?* It's Dennis that we'd like to hear about, right now. We've been listening to you for *days.*"

Brenda switched her eyes to Alec while she said that. He'd started out by looking right at Carrie, peering through his glasses with his head cocked back a little. But before she'd finished, he had turned away and dropped his chin, and started picking at a loose thread on the bedspread under him. Next to her, Elizabeth rocked slightly, side to side.

"*Anyway,*" said Carrie, turning back to Dennis. "How far *did* you get? It must have been a few *miles,* huh?"

"For sure," he said. "I don't know exactly, but I bet five miles *at least*—maybe more like ten. I was starting to get tired, man. And hungry." (Like, HALF STARVED TO DEATH.) "All I'd had *forever* was that lousy drink of soda that Marina gave me."

"You were out of town, then?" Brenda asked. "Way out there in the country when the cops showed up?"

"Yeah," said Dennis. All this time, he'd only looked at Carrie, and his feet. Now he was trying to think of what the black girl's name was. It started with a B, he knew that much. (Let's see, B, B, B . . . yeah, BRENDA. But he kept on looking at his feet, up on that table, still.) He just hoped they hadn't all decided that they hated him.

"I'm out there where it's only farms and stuff, and then this stupid cruiser comes along, and I start thinking I'm in luck. But, like I said, I hardly got into my story—how some other kids and me had gotten kidnapped and all that—and they start telling *me* I'd better go on back to Josip and Marina's and, hop in, they're going to take me back to town."

"Boy, you must have *freaked,*" said Carrie. "Finding out the cops were in on it, and everything."

Dennis shrugged. He rolled his head to look at her. "What's the point?" he said. "I just got in back—you know they don't have handles for the doors, except in front?—and they drove into town and put me in a room—I guess it was the station house they went to—and left me for a while." (For all he knew, they were going to let him ROT in there.)

"A *cell,* you mean?" said Alec. "They put you in *jail?*" Dennis had gone back to looking at his shoes.

"Nah," he said, "it wasn't what you'd call a *cell.* It didn't have a bed, or anything. Just a table and about four chairs." He paused. "The door was metal, though, and it was locked, I'm pretty sure."

"And how long did they leave you there?" said Carrie.

"Not that long," he said. "After a while, one of them came back. He had some sandwiches and milk, and he took me to the bathroom." He must have seen the look on Carrie's face, because he added, "To the bathroom *door,* that is. And when I got through eating . . . well, he let me go."

"What?" said Brenda. That seemed slightly unbelievable. Plus, she thought that Dennis hadn't been too thrilled with telling that part of the story. "They just let you go? Like that?" She snapped her fingers.

Dennis fiddled with a button on the shirt that he was wearing; it was long sleeved, made of dark blue flannel. Brenda wondered where he'd gotten it. It was much too big for him and bagged way out, even though he'd tucked it in. He'd been wearing just a muscle T, at the time he left the Winnebago; she remembered that.

"Sort of," he replied, not looking at her, still. He took his feet down off the table, and he crossed one leg; the heel of the one that wasn't crossed bounced up and down. "They told me how to get back here. I guess I told them that I would—come back here on my own, I mean. But, well, I didn't, did I?"

He finally switched his eyes to Brenda, as he asked that

question. She felt as if his doing that was like a challenge to her. But she was going to pass on that. She had no interest in a confrontation with this kid.

"I guess you *didn't*!" It was Carrie answering. She laughed. Brenda bet she knew what she'd say next. "Dumb cops! What *did* you do, instead? Go hook that shirt off someone's line?"

Brenda thought that Dennis might have looked a little shamefaced for an instant, for a flash. But then he turned his head toward Carrie once again and said, "Not quite. But close." He tried on a little laugh, and Brenda thought it fit with his expression, his whole attitude. "I got this baby from a dryer in some laundromat. But not till yesterday. I needed it. That first night, man, was *chilly*." (FROZE MY BUNS OFF is more like it.)

"Nobody took you in, I guess," said Brenda. She wanted him to get to how the other gypsies treated him, the ones who weren't cops. In light of her experience—and Alec's, she was now completely sure—she was very, very curious about old Dennis and the gypsy-on-the-street.

"Hell, no," he said. "Not that I knocked on any doors. I don't know what you'd call it, where I stayed. Both nights. There was, like, a big garage or factory, or something. And outside it were a lot of trailers? You know—the kind that trucks pull; tractor-trailer trucks? I started nosing into them, looking for a place to sleep. Well, the first two that I looked in had a bunch of big huge bales in them, made out of all these flattened cans, tin cans, and stuff like that. But in the next one, all the bales were made of *paper*, so I wiggled onto one of them and in between some others, and it wasn't all that bad a place to sleep. Although, like I said, I was a little cold—before I found this shirt."

Looking at him, Brenda had to wonder how much sleep he'd gotten, those two nights. She bet he'd been a pretty frightened child, alone in some big trailer. Except she bet there could've been some *rats* in there, as well. She shivered then and there, herself.

Dennis saw her doing that. And he smirked—the little macho man, she thought.

"But," Carrie said, "let's see—the first day you were mostly walking, right?" He nodded. "And then you're picked up by the cops and taken back, and then you found this place to spend the night . . ."

"That sounds like a big recycling center, to me," said Alec. "Bales of flattened cans, and papers. Did you see some dump trucks there, by any chance, dump trucks full of broken bottles?"

". . . but what about the *next* day, and today?" said Carrie, totally ignoring Alec. "What'd you do all *that* time?"

"Well," said Dennis, and he stretched—hands overhead, both legs straight out, together—after which he brought his heels down on the table, hard, "yesterday was when I thought I'd try to find some *kids*—you know, some people my own age. I figured kids could tell me what was going on." He grunted. "That was a disaster, though. The ones I found were worse than grown-ups, even."

With that, he told his story about looking for some kids, and finding some, all boys, out shooting baskets in some kind of park. He said he'd joined them.

"Everything seemed cool, at first," he said. "I said 'hi' and they said 'hi,' like that. They seemed all right. They weren't playing, like, a *game*—you know? Not even Horse or O-U-T, or anything. They were shooting baskets, sort of taking turns. I'm not too good at basketball, but I took off my shirt and stood around with them. But none of them would pass the ball to me."

Dennis said he figured what he'd maybe have to do was *rebound* for a while, stand underneath the hoop and pass it out to all of them. And so he did that for a good *long* while, and only after that strolled out again and took a place at one end of the foul line. But although someone else went underneath to rebound, Dennis still did not receive a pass—nor did anybody even talk to him, acknowledge he was there, in any way.

"You'd think I was invisible," he said.

Brenda hadn't had to hear that word to understand exactly what had happened there, to Dennis. He'd been ignored (that's what), the same way she had been, the same way (she was sure) that Alec was. Probably he'd also been ignored while walking up and down the different streets; he'd just been too out of it to notice that.

Dennis went on talking. Apparently, he'd started getting lippy with those kids, telling them "*My* shot," and so on. And one of them got sick of it and told him—fairly nicely, sounded like—it was a private game for just their team and that he'd better get his own ball, if he wanted any practice.

That made Dennis *really* mad, of course, and so he got into their face and told them what a lousy bunch of creeps they were—except the words he used were much, much worse—and how if any one of them, at any time, came back to where *he* lived, he'd show them how *they* dealt with such a person and et cetera. (In fact, he'd never talked like that to anyone, before.)

"Looking back," he said, "I gotta wonder why they didn't jump me. Man, I told them *good*."

Instead of jumping him, however, the other kids picked

up their ball and left the park. But not before he heard one of them say something he found very "weird," to one of his companions.

"He said," said Dennis, " 'Hey, you see? You see the way he is? We told you so.' It was like those kids not only knew exactly who I was, but also had an attitude about me. Beforehand. Before they ever even met me. I was someone they were even sort of scared of, I'm not kidding. Someone contagious with a terrible disease." He'd kind of *liked* the way they acted, actually. Afraid of him.

Hearing that, Brenda had to give the kid some credit for his sensitivity—*perceptiveness*. That was how she'd felt when she was downtown, and they all ignored her—contagious with a terrible disease.

"That's exactly how *I* felt," said Alec, breaking in excitedly. "And Brenda too, I'll bet. For some strange reason, all the people here—or all the ones we've met, except for Josip and Marina—feel a certain way about us. But what gets me is how the heck they know we're who we are—outsiders. I mean, we don't look any different from the people here. You'd think we all had scarlet letters on our . . . hey! Of course!" He held his wrist up, and he started shaking it— the wrist that had the silver bracelet on it.

"Sure." He directed that at Brenda and Elizabeth. "Our ID bracelets!" There wasn't any shutting Alec up this time. He turned to Dennis. "You were hitching, right? It wasn't till the drivers of the cars got close enough to see your wrist that they stepped on the gas—and whoosh!" He flicked his fingers out. "That's what you told us, right? That they started to slow down?" Dennis had to nod. "And also— playing basketball. They didn't see the bracelet till you took that baggy shirt off." He even spoke to Carrie, now.

Everybody in this whachacallit—country? kingdom? state?—*everybody's* in on it. They know that any kid who has a bracelet on is from the *out*side, not from Gypsyworld. A Josip and Marina import."

"He could be right," said Carrie, looking at her wrist, not him. "I should've been suspicious of a silver bracelet that's a present from a stranger, just for nothing. Especially the kind you can't get off."

"Unless you have a file," said Dennis, looking at his own. "Or real big wire cutters, maybe." (Or, like, superhuman strength, he thought, in which case you'd just flex and . . . SNAP!)

"But even if we did, so what?" said Brenda. "Bracelet on, or bracelet off, we need to figure out the answer to one big ol' question: How the heck do we get out of here? We don't even know which way to go, assuming we could dodge the cops, somehow." She looked over at the boy. "Or do we?"

"No," he said. He dropped his right foot off the table; at once, it started bouncing up and down, again. "This morning—well, I found a trailer chockful of those paper bales, and so I hid in it, just squeezed right in the back. I was thinking I could get a ride *that* way, instead of hitching. And sure enough, before too long a tractor got hitched on and off we went, my trailer and another one. We must've drove for hours."

"Yeah? And then?" said Carrie.

"Then we stopped," said Dennis. "They'd reached their destination, and they opened up the doors and there I was. They'd stopped at some big factory, it looked like. So of course they called the cops, who came and got me—same two guys. The only difference was, they didn't take my word, this time. They brought me not just *to* the door, but *through* it." And he shrugged and smirked at Brenda.

"So, all in all," said Carrie bitterly, "we aren't any better off than when we got here. Excepting for our birthday girl, who got a fish, a necklace, and a lousy peacock feather." Brenda felt the couch move, once again.

"Not necessarily," said Dennis. He looked exhausted but he got that smirk back on again.

"As soon as I came in that door, I started thinking," he went on. "Josip and Marina drove us here, all right? So what that means is they can also drive us *out* of here." If someone had asked him why he wanted that so much, why he was so intent on making his escape, on getting home, he wouldn't have known what to say, exactly. Except that, well, at home he knew what to expect. Who could tell what awful things this Gypsy King and Queen might get around to doing to them?

"All we need to do," he told the other four, "is to . . . *convince* them that they oughta. And me"—he undid a button on that baggy shirt and slid a hand inside it—"I think I've found a way to do that little thing."

The hand came out and it was wrapped around a big long pointed knife, the one Marina'd given to Elizabeth to cut her cake with. Brenda'd seen how sharp it was, the shiny silver edge it had.

ten

LOOKING AT THAT KNIFE took everybody's voice away. It wasn't just the knife itself, of course. All of them had seen a knife about that long and sharp, before. They'd seen them in their kitchens and in other people's kitchens, too. Most of them had *used* such knives to cut things with: sandwiches in half, or bagels, birthday cakes and cords on packages with knots in them that couldn't be undone. But none of them had ever seen one used for threatening another person's health and safety. They'd heard about that happening, of course; everybody had.

Carrie made the first sound. It was "Wow!" Her eyes had gotten big, and slowly, slowly, slowly, she began to nod, and smile.

Brenda didn't like the situation, not one bit. She couldn't be sure about Carrie, but *she'd* known kids who carried other kinds of knives and claimed that they would absolutely use them. And they were not the kids she hung around with.

Yet, even as she recognized her first reaction: "I don't *like* what I am seeing here," she also had a second set of thoughts. And they were: "Maybe it'd work. Maybe I can *use* this kid, this *means* that he's suggesting. Maybe he can get me home again."

When she looked across the room at Alec, she saw him straighten up and start to speak—and then think better of it. His eyes stayed on the knife. Dennis now was looking at it fondly. He scraped a thumb across its edge.

"You'd make, like, one of them, *Marina* . . ." Carrie started.

"Wrong," said Dennis, promptly. "No, I'd make *him* drive. She'd be the one I'd put this baby up against. Just maybe tickle her a little." He did a few quick corkscrew motions with his wrist that made the knife blade dance. "Cootchy-cootchy coo," he said. He was trying to remember how those hard guys did it, on TV.

"You'd use Marina as a *hostage,* sort of," Alec said. "As long as you had *her* at knifepoint, *Josip* would keep driving." Both of those were questions, Brenda thought; they just came out as statements.

"Yeah, you got it, man," said Dennis, nonchalantly. "I doubt I'd even have to prick her." And he laughed and winked at Alec. Then he tossed the knife from one hand to the other and then back again; the second toss was not a good one, and he almost caught the blade.

"But how about if Josip wouldn't even start the car?" said Brenda. "Let's suppose *she* told him not to drive us any-where, and he agreed to that."

"What?" said Dennis. He licked his lips, then slitted his black eyes and looked at her. As meanly as he could, she thought.

"Then I suppose we'd have to see what I decided, wouldn't we?" he said. "Pretty soon we'd all find out." He paused and added, "You better believe it."

"Josip'd never take the chance," said Carrie. "Josip *loves* her, you can tell that from a mile away. And besides, he doesn't know for sure how crazy Dennis is!" Laughing, she reached out and gave his arm a little shove, his empty-handed elbow.

No sooner had she touched him than the knife flicked out at her. "Cootchy-cootchy coo," said Dennis, darkly.

"Hey! For Pete's sake—*watch* it!" Carrie yelped, yanking back her hand. "You could *hurt* someone with that, you stupid little jerk-off."

"Hey—no *kidding*," he replied. "An' if you want to *prove* it to yourself, jus' keep on calling people names." He winked again and halfway smiled, then pooched his lips way out at her. Carrie gestured, rudely, back at him.

"So, what you'd do is grab Marina from behind?" asked Alec. "While she's . . . sitting at the kitchen table, maybe? Eating? Which'd mean that *Josip* would be way up at the other end?"

Brenda thought she saw what Mr. Subtle, Alec, had in mind. He was trying to put ideas in Dennis's small mind, by telling him the best and safest way to do the job, while seeming to ask questions.

"Yeah, something like that," said Dennis. He used the knife point as a toothpick, briefly, and then smiled. "Perhaps at breakfast time, tomorrow morning. No time like the present, right?" He stood and stretched. "But now I'm ready for some *sack* time, man."

"I don't want to have a thing to do with this." Elizabeth spoke up so suddenly and loudly that her seatmate, Brenda, jumped, and everybody else looked over at her.

"Well, oo doesn't *have* to," Carrie told her, speaking baby talk. "Oo can stay in her own widdle room, until her *wots*."

Then, in normal tones, "For all *we* care. One less person in the Winnebago—that won't bother *me* at all." And she stood up and started for the door.

"No, wait. Elizabeth," said Alec. "There's good reasons for the five of us to stick together. Really. It isn't all that cut and dried. Let's talk a little, after—*now*, in fact. In *your* room, if that's . . . well, okay."

"Oh, sure," said Carrie, pausing by the door. "Uh-huh, that's right, you bet. He'll want to do his talking on that widdle bed of yours, Elizabeth, you'll see. I know the kind of 'talk' *he's* got in mind."

"Oh, *Carrie*," Alec said, in a disgusted tone of voice. And, while she was coming back at him ("Sorry, Alec. I just call 'em like I see 'em"), Brenda turned and mumbled to the little girl that *she* would like to come and talk some, too. And Elizabeth had nodded, quickly.

Forty minutes later, everyone was safe in his or her own bed. But Dennis, totally exhausted, was the only one asleep. As far as what Elizabeth might do, when Dennis pulled that big knife on Marina . . . Brenda wasn't sure at all.

◆ ◆ ◆

Breakfast was, beyond a doubt, the most suspenseful meal that Brenda'd ever forced herself to eat. You could cut the tension with a knife, she thought—and then regretted thinking it. All the other kids kept half an eye on Dennis, all the time.

Josip and Marina, though, seemed more relaxed than ever. The King decided he'd make pancakes.

"They're the best thing to put under maple syrup," he explained. "Who wants to do that with me, please?"

Elizabeth and Alec said they did, Marina too, and Brenda

moments later. Dennis asked for coffee, but there wasn't any in the house, and so he took a cup of tea to go with bread that he spread peanut butter on. Carrie would have liked a jelly doughnut, but she'd asked for one before and knew they didn't have that, either. So, instead, she nibbled on a piece of toast with lots of jam on it. She would have liked to be less hungry all the time, the type "who didn't eat enough to keep a bird alive."

When the King had finished flipping pancakes and was back there in his chair (where he belonged), Brenda felt her palms get sweaty. She wiped the left one on the napkin in her lap, then put her fork down on her plate and wiped her right one.

"Oh, Dennis," said Marina, suddenly. "I find—I *have*—a flannel shirt I bet'd be your size, upstairs. Is very nice one, checks all over it. I give it to you after, if you like. Be better than that big blue item you got on, no stuff." While she said that her guests all kept their eyes fixed on their plates, and some of them forgot to breathe.

Dennis also shrugged. "This one's okay," he said.

Right after that, eyes started darting all around the table: people checking on the state of Josip's stack of pancakes, and Marina's. It seemed as if the two of them were only *bites* away from finishing, from getting up. Different versions of this thought: *Dennis chickened out* were going through four different minds.

"Dolling—is there tea, still?" Josip asked the Queen. The china pot was at the far end of the table.

Before she could reply, Dennis popped up from his place and said to her, "There is—and don't get up. I'll bring it to him."

He pushed his chair back and then walked by Carrie on

his way to where the pot was, by Marina. He even clipped her—Carrie—on the head, as he went by. But then he slid his hand inside his shirt, and two steps later he was right behind the Queen, with one hand on her shoulder and the knife point at her neck.

"Don't anybody make a stupid move," said Dennis, using what he'd learned in years of watching the tube. He was looking straight at Josip. "I don't want to have to hurt her."

Brenda was never sure of this, but she believed that someone *made* a move (smart or stupid, she was not about to judge), before the boy had even told them not to—just as the knife came out, in fact. She thought *Elizabeth* had started getting up, but that the King had grabbed her, underneath the table, grabbed her knee or thigh and forced her to sit down again. Brenda was right across the table from Elizabeth, on Josip's other side. Two things she could be certain of were: Josip's strong right arm was halfway underneath the table, and Elizabeth *had* quickly turned her head to look at him, as Dennis started speaking.

Josip answered him so calmly, so agreeably, you would have thought that Dennis had said "kiss," instead of "hurt."

"No stupid moves at *this* end of the table—is a promise," he proclaimed, holding up both open palms. "I totally surrender. Anything you say, I do. Marina also. Hey, why not? We still your friends, you see."

"You're going to take us home," said Dennis. "In the Winnebago. Take us back to where you picked us up. So find the keys. Get going. Now."

"Uh—shouldn't we all go *together*?" Alec said. "But you and Marina—sorry about this, Marina—first?"

The Queen, who hadn't moved a muscle since the boy first touched her, then said, "Not to worry, Alec. But, yes, and take some food along with, too. Is long, long drive you talk about."

"Okay," said Dennis, snappily. "Carrie! Brenda! Get some food! *Then* we'll go out to the Winnebago—me and her, and then the rest of you." He flashed his eyes at Josip. "And don't try any tricks."

The kid is on a roll, he thought. His hoarse voice sounded deadly serious; he bet no one could tell how nervous or strung out he actually was feeling. He gave the girls a head jerk—a "Get going" one.

Brenda went and got a canvas bag she'd seen inside the kitchen closet and began to put such things as bread and jam and peanut butter in it. She also found some packages of dry food—soups and cereals and so on—that she threw in. Carrie'd opened up the icebox and brought over milk and what was left of the roast chicken. There was half the birthday cake still sitting on the counter on a plate, and Brenda took that, too.

When it was time to leave the dining area, Dennis announced again that Marina and himself would lead the way, followed by the other kids and then by Josip—who had said he'd had the car keys in his pocket, all along. At almost the last minute, Dennis thought of rope, and Carrie went and got some clothesline from the kitchen closet that the canvas bag had been in. With that accomplished, it was time for "All aboard."

◆　◆　◆

The van sped smoothly out of town, but on a different highway than the one Dennis had taken, a few days before. With Carrie's help, he'd tied Marina's hands behind her back and to the bench seat that he'd had her sit on. Then, in order to make double sure she couldn't move, he told the girl to tie her ankles, too. Marina said the ropes were all unnecessary, that she "absolutely wasn't going to try no stuff," and Dennis told her sorry, but he "couldn't take no chances." There was too much "riding on it," he explained. Elizabeth sat where the Queen had sat when all of them were being brought to Gypsyworld, and Alec was back next to Brenda.

"The only trouble with this little plan"—he muttered that behind his hand, while leaning sideways, toward her ear—"is that we—none of us—know how we *should* be going. Josip could take us in the opposite direction—wherever *that* might be—or drive around in circles, and we wouldn't know it, right?"

Brenda nodded. "The only thing I know," she said, "and this is going to sound *peculiar,* is that I sort of *trust* the guy. If he can do the right thing for Marina *and* for us, I think he will."

Alec nodded. What he meant by that was "Yes, I hear you," more than "I agree." He'd just then thought that he could use the sun to make a rough determination of the way that they were heading, the *direction*. If they went around in circles, he would know *that* much, at least. Whether he'd tell Dennis (if he found that out) would be another matter. He absolutely didn't want the knife used on a person, ever. He was trying to figure out some way that *he'd* become a kind of intermediary, working out a *deal* involving Dennis and the King, bringing their two different . . . points of view together. He hadn't had much luck with that idea, so far.

Alec hoped Elizabeth was not regretting that she'd joined them in the Winnebago. The night before, when he and

Brenda'd talked to her, she'd said she thought she'd rather stay in Gypsyworld than be a party to that plan of Dennis's. He and Brenda'd argued she'd be better off coming with them and helping to keep things cool. They'd pointed out that if the Winnebago took them back to their hometown, that didn't mean she *had to* disembark. She could stay right on it, if she wanted to—return to Gypsyworld with Josip and Marina. Going on the trip would serve to keep her options open, they had said.

Alec's secret plan was that he'd talk to her some more, while they were traveling—but by himself, this time. What he hoped to do was talk her into shaking on a deal in which the two of them agreed that anything they did, they'd do together. He'd have to see if he could get her out of that front seat. Maybe she'd switch seats with Brenda. He hoped that Carrie wouldn't notice, if she did.

One thing *he* noticed, looking out the window checking on the sun, was how different every part of Gypsyworld appeared to be from anyplace that he had seen back home. Out here in the rural areas, there didn't seem to be a lot of tumbledown old houses and collapsed, decaying barns. Or little shacks with peeling paint and lots of barefoot children sitting in their dooryards. Or acreage that looked worn out and wasted. Before, on his aborted trip downtown, he'd had a set of similar impressions. There was hardly any mess, for one thing: the kind that's made by empty cans and bottles, crumpled bags and coffee cups, and candy wrappers. And wherever stuff was planted, which was everywhere, it wasn't ratty looking or half dead. People here apparently did not (for instance) drive onto the grass of neighbors' lawns or public parks, or help themselves to the flowers growing in huge pots outside stores, or break off branches from the little trees that grew between the sidewalks and the streets. He hadn't even seen a single person smoking.

♦ ♦ ♦

At the King's request, they stopped a little after noon.

"Is time for me to use the bathroom," he explained. "An' also stretch, this way and that. Driving very hard on the anatomy."

Dennis made him turn around and hand the keys to Alec, before he even left his seat.

When Josip came back from the bathroom, he suggested, "Lunch? Okay to eat a little, while we stopped here, anyway? And maybe Queen would like to also answer call of nature, eh? Why not?"

Dennis shrugged and other people nodded. Carrie knelt and got Marina's ropes untied.

"Take her to the bathroom," Dennis ordered, and Carrie walked beside the Queen up to the narrow door in back, looking not too happy, Brenda thought.

The "here" where Josip stopped the van was under a big tree that grew beside the blacktop road that they'd been driving on. For miles and miles, they'd passed by cultivated fields of grain and vegetables; on some they'd seen a tractor, pulling farm equipment of some sort, a harvester or cultivator. More recently, the level ground had given way to hills, and fields were scattered in between large stands of different kinds of trees, both leafy ones and evergreens. The field that they were going to picnic on was fenced in by barbed wire.

Brenda took the canvas bag of food and set it on some bare gray rock, atop a knoll. Alec and Elizabeth brought blankets from the van. Clearly, they were sitting in a pasture, but there weren't any animals in sight.

Everybody started asking questions of the King and Queen. How much longer they'd be driving; how far was it to the edge of Gypsyworld? They both were vague, but said it was "a good ways," still. Conversation wasn't easy. Brenda felt that everyone—and even Dennis—was a bit embarrassed by the way they'd treated Josip and Marina—by that knife routine. Marina, face it, wasn't someone who deserved to have a weapon at her neck. Or to be wrapped up in clothesline, either. Although Dennis kept the knife in hand still, he didn't make a show of it—like, wave the thing around.

Alec tried to get Elizabeth to sit off to one side, with him, and eat together as a couple. The trouble was, he asked her so darn softly that it's possible she didn't hear a thing he said. In any case, she sat beside Marina, and even shared a cup with her. They were two tin cups short, as it turned out.

Just before they got back in the Winnebago, Dennis said to Josip, "How we doin' on the gas?"

Alec, standing right by Brenda, whispered, "*I've* been wondering the same thing, for some time. I bet these things must *guzzle* gas."

"Mm-*hmm*," said Brenda, murmuring. "And I haven't seen a station for a *long* time, come to think of it. Have you?" He shook his head.

"Plenty! Fine!" boomed Josip, cheerfully. "We got two tanks on this vee-*hickle*—regular and spare. You'll see when I put in the key. We still got plenty, right? You see? And is a special kind of gas—real good."

And Dennis, after looking at the dashboard, nodded. He ordered Carrie to tie up the Queen again, but he didn't check the knots, this time.

They started down the highway, once again. Brenda thought she'd count how many cars and trucks and vans they passed, each hour. In the first one there were three, just three.

But at least they weren't going round in circles, Alec told her.

◆ ◆ ◆

Brenda wasn't one for listening to engine sounds. And so she heard the King's voice saying, "Oop-de-doop. Hey, hey! What goin' on?" *before* she was aware of what the Winnebago's motor'd started doing, which was missing. And they were going down a hill.

"Dirty frabberatz," said Josip. He pounded on the dashboard with his fist, even as he steered the Winnebago from the highway onto a small gravel road that angled off behind some bushy pines. The engine coughed, and missed, and coughed again—and then shut up for good.

"What the hell's the matter?" Dennis asked. His voice cracked, saying that.

The King was staring at the dashboard now. He'd put both hands high up there on his head of hair—the classic pose of disbelief.

"This gauge I'm looking at don't know it," he opined, "but *I* believe we out of gas!" He turned the key, experimentally; there were some engine-turning-over sounds, but nothing more than that.

"She sure not *getting* gas," said Josip.

Everybody—other than Marina and Elizabeth—reacted to the news with one or more of these: horror, outrage, anger, pain and disbelief. The Winnebago shook with questions, wailings, and demands. Nobody heard what anybody else was saying.

Dennis didn't take it well at all. He started kicking at the

Winnebago's wall and kept it up until his Reeboked toes began to *really* hurt. As he kicked, he shouted out the worst, most multisyllabled, offensive words he knew. Had he been playing in the majors, or the NBA, even the NFL, he would have long since been ejected from the premises and, most likely, fined. The league that he was in, however, didn't have a rule book.

Dennis also started crying.

"Well, look"—that was Alec, talking to (no, make that *shouting at*) the King—"how far from the border are we *now*?"

"Still a long ways." That was Josip, doing only head shakes, now, still staring at the gas gauge. "Hundred miles? At least, you bet. Two hours—more—in this vee-*hickle*. Day or two or three on foot. A lotta ups and downs."

Dennis blew his nose and screamed at Carrie, "Tie him up!" And then, at Alec, "Help her!"

Brenda'd sidled toward the back door of the van. She wasn't sure how long the King would keep on putting up with this. But she *was* as sure as sure could be that there was no way they—that pair—would *ever* tie up Josip, if he didn't feel like being tied. She also felt that any time His Highness wanted to, he could retrieve that knife from Dennis's right hand and . . . well, insert it elsewhere.

Maybe Dennis knew that, too. Keeping a respectful distance from the King, he went and put the knife against Marina's neck, again. So, pretty soon, both members of the royal couple had been tied with clothesline by the Alec-Carrie team—ankles and all hands behind their backs.

After that, debate began. There were two questions, mostly, on the floor. What to do, and what to do with *them*.

"I think you ought to kill 'em," Carrie said to Dennis,

carelessly. "Betcha anything that he did this on purpose. And if you kill 'em, we can call ourselves a buncha cutthroats—wouldn't that be neat? Keeping them around would be a great big waste of food."

Brenda didn't think that she was serious. She probably was baiting Dennis, having fun with him, taking him down a peg or two. Carrie seemed to be the type who didn't relish anyone's success for long.

"That's crazy," Alec said. "That'd be about the *dumbest* thing that we could do. It's possible we may not make it out of Gypsyworld, you know. You want to go on trial for murdering a country's King and Queen? Well, *I* don't, thank you very much." He paused. "We don't know what kind of penalties the gypsies go for. Stoning? Burning? Tearing limb from limb?" He paused again. "And anyway, I *like* the King and Queen."

"I do, too. Kill *them,* and I'll kill *you.*"

Heads swiveled toward Elizabeth. That was the first thing that she'd said to anyone, except the King and Queen, since getting on the Winnebago—and she said it quite convincingly.

Dennis looked at her with new respect.

"The chick sounds serious," he said. He didn't look like anyone about to knife someone, just then.

"Josip and Marina are the only people here who know two things I'd like to know," said Brenda. "That's where we are right now, and how do we get out of here. I vote that we untie them, feed them good, and hope they guide us to the border."

That set off more debate, and in the end it was decided to adopt the Brenda plan, except for the untying part. And further, they agreed they'd get a good night's sleep, right in their own beds in the van, and start their trek the first thing in the morning.

The King and Queen stayed very calm (again), all during the discussion. Josip said that they could sleep all right there in their big front seats, even with their hands behind them.

"Unless," he said, "our noses start in itching."

◆ ◆ ◆

How much the royal pair *did* sleep, however, is debatable. When the kids woke up, next morning, the clothes-line ropes the King and Queen had been tied up with were in pieces on the Winnebago's floor.

And Josip and Marina were . . . well, elsewhere.

eleven

❧

"LOOK!" Dennis was standing, pointing at the clothes-line pieces on the Winnebago's floor. "Great going, Carrie! You and Alec! Two IDIOTS who couldn't tie a decent knot. Not if their lives depended on it." Carrie started giggling. "That isn't funny, Carrie! I could KILL the both of you. I really could."

But Brenda noticed that he didn't have his big knife in his hand, and although he was yelling, and his voice was hoarse as usual, he didn't seem that dangerous. He looked smaller, standing by the front seats of the van, and wearing only Jockey undershorts.

Alec had his glasses on by then, and what he saw caused him to sit up in his sleeping bag, unzip the thing, and moments later tug his blue jeans on. He went and picked up pieces of the rope.

"Aha! This stuff's been *cut*," he said. He turned toward Carrie's bunk. "It wasn't that our *knots* came loose," he told her. "The knots are fine, still." He yanked the rope on either side of one. "Josip and Marina must have had a knife. Or possibly a *razor*." He made that sound real ominous.

"Let's see." Carrie left her bed and joined him. She was operating in her underwear; as usual, thought Brenda.

"You're *right,*" she said. "And whose damn fault would *that* be, Dennis? Who was meant to search them, anyway? Not me'n Alec; *we* did *our* job right. But you forgot to pat them down. *Admit* it, Dennis. *You're* the idiot, you know."

"How can *I* be sure that Josip and Marina had the knife?" asked Dennis. "Huh? Huh?" He pushed his chin out at the girl with each of those. "Who's to say"—he looked around the van—"that *Brenda* didn't cut them loose? Or Alec? Or Elizabeth?"

"Oh, sure," said Brenda, supine on her bunk, still. She made it real sarcastic. "That's *exactly* what I'd want to do. Of course. Me, who made the point that *they* were who could lead us out of here. Of course I *love* it, being lost in Gypsy-world, or God knows where, with fourteen-year-old *fools!*"

"If you want to know what *I* think," Alec said, "*I* think Josip and Marina set this whole thing up." He nodded twice, emphatically. "I'll bet they knew we had that big knife all along; I bet they missed it, putting things away. And you know what else? Josip probably screwed up that gas gauge late last night—either that or it had broken long ago, and he remembered he could trick us with it. *I'll* bet this was *their* plan, to ditch us out here in the boonies. They probably were sorry that they ever picked us up—once they saw what we were like—and this is how they've gotten rid of us." He looked around the van, checking out reactions. "They damn well ditched us," he repeated.

Brenda'd started getting up while he was talking. She really didn't care—*much* care—whose fault it was that Josip and Marina had escaped. Nor could she blame them for escaping. Alec's theory . . . that was possible, she guessed. But also less important than another thing she'd just then thought of, been *reminded* of. By this familiar feeling that she had.

"How about the *food?*" she asked, while pulling on her trousers in some haste. "Did they leave us any *food?*"

Carrie peered into the canvas bag. And then knelt down beside it, so's to fish around, inside.

"It looks to me as if," she started slowly, "as if . . . they didn't take a thing!" She shook her head. "They probably forgot, I guess. Or were in too big a hurry."

"Or maybe they decided we might need it worse than they did," said Elizabeth. She'd sat up in her sleeping bag. "Maybe they were being *nice.*" Brenda thought she sounded quite upset, in need of Mother Brenda.

"I think that's *very* possible," she said. She nodded at Elizabeth. "They'd know that *they* could hitch a ride from anyone who came along. No one's going to *not* pick up the King and Queen."

"Oh, yeah?" said Dennis. "*I* sure wouldn't. Me— supposin' they were hitchin' and I'm speedin' down the highway, hell, I'd run right over them. KA-BOOM!" He slammed a fist into an open palm.

"Yeah, supposin' that you had a *car,*" said Carrie, bitterly. "Supposin' you knew how to *drive.*" She was sulking, mad at Dennis still, for blaming *her,* her knots. She forced a laugh. "I can see *you* speeding down the highway. In a kiddy car!" She made her gesture as he pursed his lips at her.

"Well, I agree with Brenda," Alec said. "The chances are that they're a long, long way from here, already. Or even if they're not, so what? We couldn't find them if we wanted to. In any case, there's no point arguing about the King and Queen. No, the thing we'd better think about is what do we do, now?"

That shut everybody up. Alec looked extremely pleased. He now had everyone's attention.

"Let's see," he said. He dropped his head and pinched his

chin, appearing deep in thought. "It seems to me our plans would have to hinge on whether we believe that we've been going in the right direction, all along. Now, *I* believe we may have been. And so, *I'd* say we ought to keep on going—walking—following the road." (Oh, brilliant, Brenda thought.)

"But not right on the highway, Alec, right?" Elizabeth put in. "You meant we keep on going in the same direction, but, well, sort of *paralleling* where the road goes, right?"

"Damn straight," said Dennis. "I'm not getting out there where the cops'll pick me up again, I'll tell you that much, man. No walkin' in the road for me. I *know* how many strikes is out, good buddy."

Brenda thought that all of that made perfectly good sense—as good as any other thought *she* could come up with; they didn't have a ton of choices. But that hardly meant she *liked* what she was hearing. She wasn't into hiking, even *walking*. To the store or in a mall, all right. But through a bunch of woods? Forget it. And then, on top of that, try sleeping out there where a hungry wolf might come along and gobble her right up? *No way!* Except she wasn't going to have a choice. She would be Red Riding Hood, in clothing by The Gap.

"Uh—I might as well admit it," Carrie said. "I've never done much camping out. In fact, I've never spent a night outdoors. Never in my life. Not even in the park, or up on someone's roof." She cleared her throat. "I just thought I'd mention that. So no one looks at me for how to do some outdoor stuff." Of course she looked at Dennis. "I just want that understood ahead of time. *Knots* are one thing; camping out is different."

"I haven't had too much experience, myself," said Alec.

"I was in a Cub Scout troop about two weeks. I kept forgetting the salute." He produced a small self-conscious laugh. "And they were pleased when they'd forgotten *me,* I guess. Since then, I've lit the charcoal in our barbecue, but that's about the size of it."

"I'm more or less like him," said Brenda, thinking: Why get into all the gruesome details? She'd napped on some old boyfriend's blanket on the beach a time or two, and cooked a hot dog on a driftwood fire. And lost another hot dog off her stick, and into that same orange-colored flame. But actually, so what? The bottom line was that she thought she'd look ridiculous in wool-checked shirts and big ol' brogan shoes.

"Me, I'm strictly city," Dennis said. "I've started fires in a buncha trash cans—but not to cook my dinner over. Frankly, I don't see it being all that hard, this camping crap."

"It isn't," said Elizabeth. "I've spent many nights outside, and helped to cook the meals. I can make good fires, gather different foods to eat, that kind of thing. I'm not afraid of animals." She smiled. "Some of them are fairly good to eat."

People nodded nervously, after she said that, and no one looked especially delighted. To have the youngest, smallest person knowing more about . . . *survival* than the rest of them combined seemed awkward, inappropriate. Elizabeth, their leader? *Unnatural,* their faces seemed to say. Could she really have killed and eaten animals—wild animals—somewhere? Even Alec didn't look as if he'd go for that.

"Well. Maybe we should make a pile of all the stuff we're going to carry," he suggested. "How does that sound? Put it right beside the van, there." He pointed to a spot, outside the door. "And then we can divide it up. In loads. Of different sizes, I suppose."

Elizabeth stood up and nodded; Alec looked relieved.

Half an hour later, everyone was outside staring at the things they'd taken from the van. It wasn't such a huge collection: all five sleeping bags, the food, a frying pan, a pot, tin plates and cups, utensils from the kitchen. Also matches and a first-aid kit, a plastic tarp, two rolls of toilet paper (all there were), salt and pepper shakers and the clothes-line pieces that they'd used to tie the King and Queen.

"Shouldn't we eat something *now?*" said Carrie, who was hungry. "Carry some of this *inside* us?"

"Right," said Brenda, "and I vote we start with spoil-ables. That chicken there, for instance. And the milk." She'd gotten sick on nasty chicken, once—had thrown up half the night.

"If we take small bites and chew them slowly," said Elizabeth, "we'll probably eat less. And that would be a good idea, I think. We don't have very much, here. No-where near enough for three days worth of walking."

That made everybody do things with their lips and stare at what they had, the food part of it. There (really) *wasn't* very much: three quarters of a loaf of bread and half a birthday cake, some peanut butter, jam, six envelopes of soup and noodle mixes, plus some cereal and rice and two small bags of pinto beans—that, and the remainder of the milk and chicken.

"Of course, I'm sure we'll find some other things to eat and drink," Elizabeth continued. She sounded cheerful. "Roots and nuts and berries. And there seem to be a lot of brooks around." She didn't mention animals, a lot of people noticed.

Brenda noticed everybody watching everybody else, as they ate breakfast—doing pig patrol. And for the moment, anyway, everyone was taking little helpings, being good team players. She tried, herself, to nibble at her food, eat slower, chew a lot.

Dennis, who'd retained the big long knife—had it in his belt, in fact—cut himself a very tiny sliver of the birthday cake.

"For energy," he told the group, as he broke off a little bit and put it in his mouth. "I need that sugar, man. I'm glad that you got born, Elizabeth."

After he said that, he did his kissy thing at Carrie, one more time. And this time she smiled back at him.

♦   ♦   ♦

By five o'clock that afternoon, however, no one in the group was smiling much. Elizabeth believed they'd walked no more than fifteen miles but, as the King had said, a lot of it was up and down, and both of them were hard on legs and feet that weren't used to them.

They'd tried to keep the road in sight; that wasn't easy, though. At times it was impossible. For the most part, they were walking in the woods; trees limited the distance they could see. And, too, they sometimes took the path of least resistance, meaning that they went *around* a swamp, instead of through it, even if that took them farther from the road and made them circle back to find it. All day, they heard only four cars go by.

They'd started out by walking for three hours straight, before they stopped for lunch. *Mistake,* as it turned out. When they'd finished eating, no one was real eager to get up and start again. Elizabeth suggested taking rests, each hour, after that, "just for—oh, five minutes." Everybody said that sounded like a great idea. On their first such stop, the little girl lay flat before a tree and stretched her legs straight up on it, heels high up on its trunk.

"What are you doing *that* for?" Carrie asked, suspiciously.

"Good for circulation," Elizabeth replied. "Your legs feel better, after."

"Well," said Brenda, "I'll try anything." She did, and at the next break everyone was doing that same thing. As Brenda said, "They don't feel *that* much better, but at least they don't feel too much worse." By five p.m., though, she wasn't saying that, not anymore. She was ready for the end of it, this rotten day. It was time to stop somewhere and spend the night there. She'd *almost* gotten up the nerve to say that.

But of course she didn't. Stopping for the night would be, in certain ways, much worse than walking. For one thing, once they'd stopped, there wasn't—wouldn't be—the slightest possibility of seeing (over that next rise of ground) the *border,* a *motel,* their *parents,* or (a real long shot) the *U.S. Cavalry.* Once they stopped that meant they'd be *there* for the night. And the only "theres" that Brenda'd seen so far were certain to become, when it got dark, the kinds of places she'd prefer to *never* spend a night in—places lacking roofs and walls and any of the things her mother called "conveniences."

Ahead of her, Elizabeth had halted and was leaning up against a tree. She was looking down a little slope, and at the small brook at the bottom of it.

"How about we camp right here?" she said. "Who knows where the next stream's going to be?"

"Looks good to me," said Alec, promptly.

"I'm ready to put down this sucker," Dennis said, holding up the big black fry pan from the Winnebago. He'd lugged it all the way, made it his responsibility. He had noticed that it wouldn't fit in any of the packs they'd all constructed out of pillowcases and some lengths of clothes line—copying the one Elizabeth had made.

"Yeah, I want to take my shoes and socks off," Carrie said. "Soak my tootsies in that water for a while. My feet are burning up, no kidding."

Brenda sighed, resignedly. "Guess we might as well," she said, and started down the slope. Already, she was planning how she'd make it through the night.

Elizabeth, she thought, would make a fire. *She* would put her sleeping bag as close to it as possible, even at the risk of getting overheated. Wild animals, like wolves, were scared of fire. Even more than she was scared of them, she hoped.

◆　◆　◆

Brenda didn't fall asleep for quite a while, that night—for *hours,* she was pretty sure. Everybody else had gone to sleep before she did. The reason she was sure of that was no one answered to her last few "What was *that?*"s. At first, Elizabeth had told her what it was ("The wind." "A tree branch." "Sounded like an owl." Etc.). And later, different people started saying, "*Shut up,* Brenda, will you?" The fire'd burned real low before she fell asleep, but she'd been much too scared to get out of her sleeping bag to feed it.

When she woke up again—sure she'd only been asleep for *minutes*—it was light out, and the other kids were still asleep. She was hungry, and she also had to go; without the dark, it wasn't really scary, anymore. And so she wiggled from her sleeping bag and put on all the things she'd taken off the night before: her left shoe and the right one. Then, biting back a groan of *total* body pain, she climbed the little slope behind their camp, heading for some private place to pee.

With that accomplished, she decided—oh, brave girl!—she'd walk a little ways upstream and splash some water on her face. When she'd gone . . . oh, maybe fifty yards, and around a little bend, she found a pool that looked to be about knee deep, and sandy bottomed. *Perfect!* And then, because as if on cue, the sun popped out and everything looked warm and bright and cheerful, she asked herself why not slip off her clothes and splash some water *everywhere*—take a morning *dip*? Why not, indeed? She grinned. She found the thought *exciting,* even. Swimming naked in a mountain stream? How *daring*—how old fashioned! Oh, Lord—her friends at home would *flip*! Provided that they ever got to hear about it.

The water was quite cold—like, *freezing,* really—cold enough to drink without an ice cube in it; but she still went in. "Swimming" was a slight exaggeration, maybe, but she did sit down, then stretch out on her back, right in the middle of the pool. And quickly, afterward, leap straight up on her feet again, gasping still for breath, her hands clasped underneath her chin.

But the air was warm, and pretty quickly she felt *great,* exhilarated by her dip. And so she took another, even dunking her whole head, this time, and wiggling her underwater arms and legs. And when she stood back up, she felt so proud and good—and beautiful! She felt like yelling, telling everyone how *perfect* that cold water was.

It was as she waded out that she first heard the whistling. Some song she knew, but didn't know the name of. That told her someone else had gotten up; she wondered who. And even though she knew that he or she had seen her in her birthday suit before, she jumped up on the bank and mopped her body with her shirt a bit, then quickly got all dressed again.

The whistling continued, but not getting any closer, and as she finished dressing she was hit by something: it was coming from the wrong direction! That had to mean, she thought, that someone else had gotten up and also gone upstream, but even farther, and was maybe having his or her own dip up there. Brenda blushed; that person, very probably, had seen her on the way.

Well, to hell with them, she thought; *she* had looked all right.

She smiled. Two could play at Peeping Tom, and it was her turn, now. She wouldn't show herself, not right away. And then, depending on the person that it was, she'd either say hello, or . . . *growl*! She could just imagine Carrie jumping—or Dennis with his hair straight up on end. She grinned again and clambered up the slope. Using all its trees for cover, she started moving upstream.

Well, she saw the mule before she saw another living thing, and almost passed out on the spot. A mule—or donkey, burro, big-eared minihorse—was standing by itself just eating grass and minding its own business, but—a *mule*?

And closer to the brook there was a dog that looked to be asleep, a little collie sort of dog.

And hunkered down beside the fire he'd just started, whistling again, there was a boy. But not just any boy—*the* boy. The one she'd last seen in the dark of night, sneaking into Josip and Marina's.

twelve

BRENDA WAS AFRAID. Her first reaction was to be afraid. Being in the woods and seeing him in such a setting, that was part of it. The woods were full of trees and stuff that she not only didn't know the names of, but that also'd never had a thing to do with *her*. The woods were fine for animals and . . . Indians, but she could do without them very nicely, thank you. She was in the woods, in Gypsy-world, and trying to get back home, and here was someone who she didn't really trust or even *know*. (Whether she might *like to* was another matter, altogether.)

The only people who she *sort of* knew, who she could *sort of* trust, were those four other kids who also wanted to go home again—except for, possibly, Elizabeth. Anybody else—surely any *gypsy*—was potentially a problem. And more so ever since the moment Dennis pulled that knife on Josip and Marina.

This boy—young man—who she was looking at was certainly a gypsy. And absolutely all mixed up in all of what was going on, somehow. This was the third time that she'd seen him. (Brenda felt her heart beat, rapidly but strongly; she was feeling less afraid.) The day she'd talked to him, she'd *thought* he seemed to be a decent, caring person—in addition to nice looking. (Which he was now, still, attired in a crimson woolen shirt and olive pants and leather boots, over six feet tall, broad shouldered with a lean, athletic build. She thought he must be from an *island,* a place where different sorts of people came together, once upon a time. Dark and curly haired and heavy browed, he had a prideful, gentle look, like someone very much at peace with who and how he was: a person you could count on, who could do it all.) But he hadn't helped her; *au contraire,* he'd fled, aboard a bus. And then he'd come to Josip and Marina's house that very night, had *snuck* in, when she should have been asleep. He'd known that she was there, because she'd told him that, downtown. Yet, clearly, he had *not* come to the house in order to see *her*. (To hell with him, she thought.)

But here he was, again. It seemed as if it *couldn't* be an accident, or a coincidence, that they were in the same vicinity, *again*. But what else *could* it be? He had some kind of *jackass* with him, and a dog. You don't go saddle up a jackass, if you're chasing people down, and she'd never heard of dropping donkeys, wearing parachutes, from planes. So there was no way he could possibly have followed them (come after her), in other words.

Staying in a crouch, Brenda very slowly turned around and *tiptoed* through the woods, away from where she'd been. She could still hear whistling behind her; she was sure he hadn't heard (or was ignoring) her.

Brenda went quite quickly back to where the other four were sleeping, still. The only (smart and safe) thing they could do, she thought, was leave the area as rapidly as possible. The alternatives (regrettably) were just too dangerous.

No longer was it even in her mind to brag about the fact that she'd gone *swimming,* in an ice-cold mountain stream.

♦   ♦   ♦

"Come *on*! Let's move it, people. Time's a wasting, here."

Ten minutes later, Brenda, with her sleeping bag rolled up and stuffed inside her pack, and it slung over her left shoulder and the big black fry pan in that hand, was whispering—*stage* whispering—those words. And, moments later, *whining* others like them, especially to Carrie.

If such a thing were possible (thought Brenda), Carrie'd gotten up out of the wrong side of the ground, that morning; she was even crankier, and foggier, than usual.

"What?" she'd say. And *"Where?"* And then, of course, "Who did you say he is?" followed by "How old?" and other stupid, irritating things like that till Brenda could have conked her with that frying pan. *Would* have, too—if she had been a different kind of person.

She'd decided not to tell the others that she'd seen the boy *before*. To do so, she believed, would only slow things down and complicate them, too. Alec, at the very least (and Carrie, too, if she knew Carrie), would demand to know the reasons why she hadn't mentioned him before. And, well, she really couldn't say. (Wouldn't-couldn't, what's the diff? she asked herself.) "None of your business," which she might have *felt* like saying, would have surely brought about some time-consuming arguments and conflicts. And besides, she didn't talk like that. Too often.

Carrie finally got her high-tops on, with all the laces laying flat, the way she liked them to. And then she struggled to her feet, as everybody else had (long since) done. All she had to do was roll her sleeping bag and get it in her pack;

Elizabeth, to help her out, had put her fair share of the other stuff—food, et cetera—in it, already.

And then the cawing started. "Cawing" as in crow sound.

In the silence of the woods it sounded very loud. It was also unexpected. They had all heard crows before. Along with robins, eagles, pigeons and canaries, crows were birds that all of them were pretty sure they could identify, at least in pictures. But they hadn't all heard crows that near, or that persistent.

"Caw, caw, caw!" this crow kept screaming. "Caw, caw, caw, caw, CAW!"

Everybody looked in the direction of the racket. Dennis even pointed, claiming that he saw the stupid thing, up in some tree or other. It was on the upstream side of them, somewhere up the slope.

"Come *on*," said Brenda, one last time. "Let's *go*." She wasn't interested in bird watching.

There was another sound, though, up the slope: the crackling of leaves and little branches, the noise a person or an animal would make, while walking through the forest.

"Allo!" A voice rang out, a happy, young man's voice. "Hey—lookit all of you! Good grief! Allo allo allo *allo!*"

◆ ◆ ◆

He'd said he was Francisco, but called "Cisco," as a rule. He was sitting on a log. The dog, who'd followed him quite closely down the slope, had flopped down at his feet.

It was a Shetland collie, a long-haired shaggy little guy whose coat was black and brown and white. He looked extremely on the ball, and curious. The kids, who God knows were *extremely* curious themselves, got grouped around Francisco in a circle, Alec sitting on the ground,

Elizabeth and Dennis leaning on two trees, Carrie kneeling on her sleeping bag, and Brenda sort of hovering around.

And the *crow,* amazingly, had swooped down from a tree and landed on Francisco's shoulder. It now was shifting weight from foot to foot and fixing each kid with its beady eyes, in turn.

Cisco was performing introductions.

The dog's name was McDuff (although he'd also answer to plain Duff or Duffy); he was a Scottish gypsy, Cisco said. (And Duffy thumped his tail, agreeably.) The crow was "Jackie"; she *claimed* to be a jackdaw, Cisco said, descended from a family that lived in only haunted, ruined castles, back in Europe. Cisco said he thought the crow was lying, that she was a *Corvus brachyrhynchos,* related to the jackdaw but completely North American, a resident of trees.

When he said that, the crow began to mutter something, sticking its large beak inside the neckband of Francisco's red wool shirt, not pecking at him, just *invading* him a little.

"And over where I camped is Babylon," said Cisco, "who's a donkey or, to be exact, a Mesopotamian ass. She lords it over all of us, because she's from about the oldest family of anyone. She says they go back to the dawn of history. Carried seedlings for the Hanging Gardens, and all that." Cisco beamed around the circle.

"So that is us," he said. "Now who the *hell* are all of you?"

Alec, naturally, presided, naming each of them in turn. Cisco rose and went around the circle, shaking everybody's hand, saying he was pleased to meet each one. Brenda wasn't used to having someone near her age do that, but she noticed that his hand was strong and warm—that he surely did feel capable.

Cisco said that he was working as a census taker, but he

wasn't counting people. His interest was in all the plants and animals living in this "agroforest" (as he called it). He said that other than the people who were working in the area, and who lived in little settlements where he would go to get supplies, he hadn't seen another human face in two months' time.

As he told that *whopper* of a lie, he looked at Brenda, squarely and directly, and the look said, "Trust me. Please."

She turned away, not wanting him to try to read her face, her answer. The one inside her heart was not "I do"—or "Hell, no," either. It was, absolutely, "Maybe."

"And *you*-all?" Cisco said. "What brings you way out here? You aren't gypsies, I don't think. Or are you?"

There was a silence in which eyes went off in all directions. Finally, Alec said, "You didn't see our bracelets?" And he held his wrist up.

Cisco said, "Yeah, sure. I saw them. What are you, then, some kind of team from somewhere? Or a *club,* or something?"

"In a way," said Brenda, suddenly, deciding she could play some version of his game—why not? Mix a teaspoonful of truth with one full cup of lies, and stir, and serve as long as people swallow it.

"We're all from different schools," she said, "outside of Gypsyworld, and members of our student governments. And, well, you see, the area Jaycees have sort of sponsored us—our trip? It's like a *project* that we're doing." She was getting into stride. "When we get back, we're meant to, like, *report* to our communities on everything we've learned in Gypsyworld. About how different things are done, compared to home. And what, if anything, we have to learn from them—you—*here. You* know. And maybe vice versa."

As she finished saying that, while looking at Francisco, Brenda could see Carrie, from the corner of her eye. Using just one hand, she looked like someone playing in a sandbox, filling up a little pail.

"I *see*," said Cisco. He looked at her and nodded; he looked *fascinated*, Brenda thought. "That's interesting. And you are in the woods, this agroforest here, to *study* it? I'd be extremely interested to hear—" His eyes were twinkling.

"Wait," said Dennis. Brenda could have kissed him for the timely interruption; now there's a Famous First, she thought. "How come you didn't think we were from Gypsyworld? You say it wasn't 'cause you saw we had these bracelets on?"

"No, not at all," said Cisco. He was back to smiling openly, again. "It was . . . please don't take this wrong, your *sneakers,* if you want to know the truth. Your sneakers and your packs. Every one of you has got a different kind of sneaker on, and some of them so fancy! *Spiffy!* Yes. Good grief." He laughed, as he said that. "But no one's got a halfway useful pack. Don't get mad, but, well, to me they look like *pillowcases*."

"Uh, yes," said Brenda quickly. "That's exactly what they *are*! On account of something else our sponsors wanted us to do while we were here: survival camping. The idea was for us to beg or borrow different ordinary household things and, like, *adapt* them." She had no idea if that was plausible, or not. *Survival camping? Please.* "Isn't that right, Alec?"

"Um—absolutely," Alec said. He felt that he'd been called upon unfairly, but he also wanted—needed—to come through. "What we are, is on our way back home. This survival camping deal is meant to be the last . . . *component* of our trip, the thing we do while . . . *trekking* to the border.

We'd been staying with the King and Queen, you know. With Josip and Marina. It was them who lent us all this stuff and dropped us off out here."

Dennis started coughing; Brenda nodded solemnly. That Alec (she was thinking), he could play the game himself. Not bad at all, she thought. And Alec didn't even know that *Cisco* knew that they'd been staying with the King and Queen.

"Oh, really?" Cisco said. "You stayed with Josip and Marina? Lucky you, I'd say. They're two amazing people."

"Yes," Elizabeth piped up. "We thought they were the greatest."

"Our only trouble now," said Alec, "is that *stupidly*—and this is my fault, I'm afraid—we left the map they gave us in the van." He shook his head and looked down at the ground. "So we're a little lost, right now."

"Hmm," said Cisco. "Sounds as if you're going to need some help, then. The border's quite a ways from where we are right now."

"Yes," said Brenda. "Yes, exactly. We could really use another map." She paused. "Or something."

"Well, *gee,*" said Cisco. Brenda almost rolled her eyes; things were starting to get *over*done. "It just so happens that *we're* following the route you want to take, almost exactly. We don't go fast, or straight, because we've got some work to do—and 'fast' is not in Babylon's vocabulary—but I know we're going to get there."

"How far from there—the border—are we, anyway?" asked Dennis. "Starting from right here."

"As the crow flies?" Cisco said. "Let's see. Maybe fifty miles. Not all that far. Except that, like I said, we won't be going straight." He turned to the black bird. "Wouldn't you say fifty, Jackie? Straight up to the border?" He smoothed its feathers with his fingers.

The bird appeared to think that over. She cocked her head, both left and right. And then she nodded—deeply, gravely—once.

"So, how'd you like to join me?" Cisco said.

Brenda waited, wanting someone else to say and knowing that she wouldn't have to wait for long. She just hoped he knew which answer was the right one. From *everybody's* point of view, of course.

"Sure, why not?" said Dennis. Brenda had expected Alec's voice, so she was startled, almost, for a moment there. Carrie shrugged and Alec looked at Brenda and Elizabeth; both of them were nodding.

"Fine, if you don't mind," said Alec, diplomatically.

Cisco grinned. "Heck, I'd like the company. Maybe you can help me with the work." He stood and stretched; the bird flew off his shoulder. "So, suppose I go and eat my breakfast and pack up my camp? That shouldn't take but . . . oh, a half an hour, probably."

"Okeydoke," said Brenda. "Perfect."

◆　◆　◆

As soon as he was out of earshot, almost everybody started talking, all at once.

"I hope that was all right," said Alec, looking like he *knew* it was. "My saying that about our having stayed with Josip and Marina. And about the map, and all."

"Sure," said Carrie. "I thought everything that everybody said seemed really *smart*. Except when *Dennis* started coughing, like an idiot." But the way she looked at him, you could tell she didn't mean it.

He grinned and pulled that knife out of his pack, and started waving it around, again.

"Maybe what we ought to do is hold this baby on ol' *Cisco,*" Dennis said. "Tie him up and take his food and stuff. His donkey, too." He winked at Carrie, grinning. "That way you could get home sitting on your ass." He laughed, a little louder than the joke demanded, Brenda thought.

"Don't be ridiculous," she said, just in case the kid was serious. "We need a guide as much or more than we need food. This is a really lucky break, running into somebody as out of it as this guy is."

Elizabeth was smiling. "Me, I really like the crow," she said.

thirteen

IN THE FIRST THREE DAYS that they were traveling with Cisco, Alec, Brenda, Carrie, Dennis and Elizabeth learned a lot of things about the guy—things both strange and interesting, some of which, at times, to some of them, were also quite discomforting.

Here's a little sampling, from all their mental lists:

- He certainly had told the truth when he'd informed them, "We don't go fast, or straight . . ." (A, B, C, D, E—that's *everyone*—became aware that *that* was so).
- He absolutely *loved* what he was doing (B and E both noticed).
- He could make the ax work that he did—cutting, splitting, trimming—look as if it was a cinchy little job that anyone could do, *which it absolutely sure as hell was not* (D).
- The only person who seemed to actually see a lot of the things he pointed at was Elizabeth (A and B), but he still pointed at about a million different items—animal and vegetable and mineral—per hour (A, B, C, D, E).
- He—stupidly—liked Brenda best (C).

- He looked at, picked up, measured, counted and made notes on about a thousand different things a day (A, B, C, D, E). Which seemed like overdoing it (A, B, C, D).
- He cared about the animals, Duff and Babylon and Jackie, just as much as, or even *more* than, any of the humans in the group (B).
- He could swim, not great, but good enough, without a bathing suit (A, B, C, D, E), which made not knowing how to even more embarrassing (D), and which probably made it all right for other people to go skinny-dipping, too (C).

♦ ♦ ♦

"We're going to stay among the trees the first few days," he'd told them as they started out. "Neat-o, right? *Enjoyable*. An' besides, we got no better friends than these big plants." He went and put his arms around the trunk of one, a straight young maple.

Brenda stared at him, determined that she'd keep an open mind on . . . everything. She would try to take an interest in his interests; everybody knew that that was sort of basic to the making of a good relationship. She'd never thought of trees as *plants* before, but she supposed they were. Their stems were made of wood because they *had to* be; unless it had a hard strong stem, a plant that size would fall right over. So, she'd picked up a brand-new, interesting fact: trees are big old plants.

"I s'pose you student council smarties all know what this baby here is good for," Cisco said. He slapped the maple's rough gray bark. "I mean, *aside* from syrup, sugar, furniture and climbing when you got a wild boar on your tail. And shade." He looked around the group, a broad smile on his face, a broad *expectant* smile.

"Um, seems to me I heard that trees—or maybe growing plants in general—take in a lot of . . . *something*," Alec said.

"Yeah, *water*—duh," said Dennis. "Birds."

"No, no, a *gas*," said Alec. "Or an element?"

Now Cisco had a *wary* look, the kind that people have when they suspect they're being kidded.

"Carbon," he began. "They absorb a lot of CO_2—

"Carbon dioxide," Carrie interrupted, gleefully. She took a breath and opened wide and, leaning, blew it out at Dennis, who seized his nose and throat while making strangled sounds.

". . . which means it don't layer out up there in space and help to make it like the inside of a greenhouse, here on Gypsyworld or Earth."

"Yeah, who'd want flowers, all year round?" said Carrie. "And *not* have any snow days in the winter? Wear shorts all the time?" She made a face. "Oh, *horrors!*"

"Well, actually," said Alec, "if it got to be that warm— that *nice*, you *could* say—where we are, it'd be unbearable down south, I guess."

"Not with air conditioning," said Dennis. "Probably, by then, they'd have these air conditioners, no bigger than a Walkman, maybe. Everybody'd have one, and they'd walk around with it and have their own cool space."

"Yeah, cool," said Carrie. She swayed and snapped her fingers. She thought this was a stupid conversation. "And anyway, who cares about a bunch of southerners?"

"You might," said Elizabeth, "if they marched up to your house with guns, and told you they were going to live there, now."

"Impossible," said Dennis. "That's what we have an army for. To make sure that crap like that don't ever happen."

Brenda kept her eyes on Cisco while those others chitter-chattered back and forth. At first, he looked like someone waiting for a joke to end, a joke he isn't sure that he is following. But then he shrugged and turned away, picking up the walking stick he'd laid down on the ground. Clucking to the donkey, Babylon, he started heading upstream, looking for a place to cross, as it turned out. Brenda and the others took the clue and followed him. Walking through the woods, everybody soon ran out of guns-and-army talk.

◆　◆　◆

Brenda'd watched the evening news on the TV, sometimes. Her parents always did; they said it was a person's duty to "keep up on things." And so the words "greenhouse effect" were perfectly familiar to her. They went with "global warming," and she knew that both of them were bad.

One time, she'd seen this graphic on the news: it showed a drawing of the globe, with the North Pole and the South Pole regions both in white. And then it showed the globe as it was getting hit by rays that made the areas of snow and ice start melting. And after that, it switched to showing how a lot of parts of different countries would be underwater if the melting polar ice increased the oceans' level, some. All the shapes of all the continents got really different, when that happened.

Brenda frankly doubted that it ever would, though. She'd even asked her social studies teacher, Mr. Simpson, what *he* thought. He was the coolest of the young white teachers at her school; he drove a sporty little coal-black Honda, with some real good sound in it. What he said was that he thought that long before the oceans started rising, the scientists'd figure out some way to make damn sure they didn't.

"They'll come up with new technology, or something," Mr. Simpson said. "They always have and, mark my words, they always will. I'm not going to sweat it, I can tell you that much." And he winked.

"But, hey," he said, "I'll get myself a Chris Craft if I have to." And everybody'd laughed as he made powerboating motions with his hand.

◆ ◆ ◆

It didn't take two days for everyone to fall in love with Duff, and Babylon, and Jackie. Brenda, frankly, was surprised when *she* did. The only pet she'd ever had before had been a little turtle that had disappeared one day; she'd thought her mother might have vacuumed it. But all of Cisco's three were much more fun to be around than her old turtle had been. They sort of made you think about . . . well, how it was to *be* an animal, and realize how *neat* they are. It also made her think about how she had never paid attention to that turtle.

Duffy was a dog who liked a lot of contact. And he played no favorites, getting it. Anytime there was a rest stop, or a meal, he'd come and sit beside (you could say *with*) a different person, and slowly he'd edge closer and still closer till at last he actually was leaning up against that person's leg. If the person chanced to pat his head, or scratch behind his ear, he'd look up at them adoringly and close his eyes. Moments later, he'd flop down and go to sleep.

Carrie found him irresistible. Almost every time he walked in her direction—tongue lolling out and eyes alight and smiling, with his bushy tail in motion—she'd cry out, "Oh, Duff!" and drop down on her knees and throw her arms around his neck, burying her face in his thick ruff.

Dennis liked to mock the baby talk that Carrie spoke to him, sometimes.

"Wooza wooza wooza," he would say, pretending he was her, pretending (too) that he was so above that, such a stud. But Brenda wasn't fooled. She'd been watching him with Babylon.

First night out, Cisco'd given Dennis two small carrots from his food supply and suggested he might like to feed them to the donkey. Dennis didn't look too thrilled by that suggestion, but he took the things and offered one to Babylon. The way he did it was a riot, Brenda thought. He almost looked like someone in a relay race: one arm stretched straight out as far as possible, but all the rest of him prepared for takeoff, in the opposite direction—just in case old Babby snapped.

Well, of course she didn't; she was a dainty eater. She took the carrot gently in her big front teeth, holding it at first as if it was an eggshell. Five minutes later, Dennis could be seen with one arm thrown around her neck, his mouth right up against her twitching ear.

"You know"—he turned and said to Cisco—"she smells *good*." And with that he rubbed his stubby nose against her velvet cheek.

Alec seemed to go for all the animals, although (he once told Brenda) his father hated pets and they had never had "a guppy, even" in his house. He liked to hike beside the donkey, with a hand out on her mane or bridle. Brenda thought that this was partly for the sake of balance—Alec being such a spaz—but she also felt he valued the uncomplicated friendship of the animals, how neither Babylon nor Duffy ever looked at him with pity or disgust. And how both of them would follow where he led them.

Elizabeth could not get over Jackie. First thing in the morning, she'd slide out of her bed—or, anyway, her sleeping bag—and call to her.

"Jackie Jackie Jackie!" she'd cry out, sounding like some kind of bird, herself, almost, and holding up her hand and spinning in circles, trying to see way up into the trees.

In hardly any time at all, the crow would hear and be there, swooping in and circling and slowing, till she gently came to rest right on the waiting hand.

Then, Elizabeth would get a cookie out of Cisco's pack, a cookie that the crow would reach out with her beak and take. With this huge prize now in her mouth, she'd flutter to the ground. There, she'd break it more or less in half and eat the larger piece, nodding at Elizabeth between each bite, as if to say, "Good stuff!"

But after she was finished eating, she had more to do. She'd take the other piece and hop along a little ways with it, until she found the perfect place to lay it down. Having done that, she would look around and find a *leaf,* a good-sized one, which she would place, with care, right on the cookie fragment. Then she'd hop away and check her work, making sure there wasn't any cookie showing, that it was completely hidden by the leaf. If it wasn't, she would make adjustments; if it was, she'd nod and do a little knee bend so as to push up off the ground, and fly, and disappear amid the branches overhead. Moments later, she would "Caw caw caw."

"*Real* good manners," said Elizabeth.

"Jackie likes it better when we get out of the trees," Cisco said to her. "The stuff a crow prefers to eat the most—besides an oatmeal cookie—they can find the easiest in fields. Crow treats are really pretty gross: beetles on the half shell, anything (like toads or mice) a tractor wheel ran over. In fact, they love to eat, alive . . . well, anything that runs when kitchen lights go on. It's not always easy, Jackie says—killing moles or cleaning up a pile of something-guts—but someone's gotta do it. Nature needs its trash collectors, its disposals." He wrinkled up his nose, and grinned.

"That's right," said Alec, walking up and overhearing. He'd gone down to the brook they'd camped beside the night before (they always camped near water), and he must've slipped as he knelt down to wash his face. His trouser legs, the fronts of them, were soaked from knees on down. "You always see them on the highway, pecking at what used to be a skunk, before some yahoo bonked it, going sixty-five."

"Well, here in Gypsyworld, there isn't that much road kill," Cisco said, "because we drive so little, as compared to you. And, of course, we go much slower, too."

"I noticed," Brenda said. "You seem to have a lot more bikes than trucks or cars. By far." She was crouching down beside their fireplace, stirring powdered milk and chocolate squares into some water in their kettle. The idea was to end up with hot cocoa. Cisco hadn't taken tea, she'd noticed, and she thought he might enjoy a nice hot cup of cocoa.

"And aren't gypsy cars *electric,* some of them?" asked Alec. "I mean, I noticed that they kind of *buzz* along, instead of sounding like a car."

"The trouble with electric cars," said Dennis, "is that they're too much like a horse and buggy. They got no power, man, no pep, no range. They got no style, no shape, no pull on me whatever, batteries included. What the chicks put out for is something like a new Trans-Am. You just ask Carrie." And he laughed. Dennis was wondering if somebody—one of the ones who knew how to cook—was going to make something for breakfast. Like hot cereal, or eggs, or pancakes. At the moment it appeared he'd have to settle for another peanut butter sandwich.

"Yeah," said Cisco, "and you know what those *Trans-Ams* put out? All four hundred million of them—that's including all their relatives that run on gas and oil? Five hundred and fifty million tons of carbon, every year. Five hundred fifty million *tons,* my friend. Good grief, just think about it. Five hundred fifty million tons of *stuff,* right out of all their tailpipes, up into the atmosphere. That's a huge part of the greenhouse deal, right there." He shook his head and sipped out of the cup that Brenda'd handed him.

"I thought you said that trees take care of that," said Brenda. "That they, like, eat the carbon up."

Cisco smiled. "They would," he said, "except, outside of Gypsyworld, you dopes are cutting them and burning them. Worldwide, you've lost about a fifth of all the forest that you used to have—oh, forty years ago. And back in 1600 there was forest *everywhere.*"

Suddenly he stopped and raised a finger.

"Hey, listen up," he said. "You guys hear that? That was something you used to have all over, when the Pilgrims came. But then you hunted them so hard, you almost wiped them out. That was a big wild turkey."

"Wait," said Carrie. "That's not fair. I don't think the turkeys here in Gypsyworld are half as big and wild as *any* of the ones we've got, back home. Just take the specimen we brought along with us. We call him 'Alec,' right? She gestured in the guy's direction. "Isn't he a beauty?"

"What?" said Alec. "What? You calling *me* a turkey, woman?" He started lurching toward her, with his elbows sticking out and flapping in a way he must have thought was turkey-style. "Perhaps I'll gobble you right up."

"EEEK!" cried Carrie, feigning terror. "Help me, somebody! The *turkey's* going to get me." She began to laugh. "And he's going to *gobble* me!"

She began to shriek in mock hysteria and, very soon, in mild discomfort. Alec, with his hand made into turkey claws, was trying to tickle her, but not succeeding very well.

"Here," said Brenda, coming to the rescue, "maybe I can use my cocoa to distract him." She advanced on Alec, holding out another cup of what she'd made.

"Cocoa?" Cisco said. "So *that's* what this stuff is!"

Which, naturally, got Brenda shrieking, too.

fourteen

❧

UNTIL THE FOURTH DAY, Brenda never got a chance to be alone with Cisco. Oh, there'd been *moments* when the two of them were by themselves—washing dishes, say—but those had been short lived. Even washing dishes, they'd look up to find that someone had come stumbling or mumbling along to join the party. Or at least to give advice, or criticize, or bring a heavily encrusted pot or pan they had "forgotten."

But, on the fourth day, Cisco said he had to mark some trees that would be "harvested" (he said), later on that month. He'd explained to them that trees continue to absorb the carbon in the atmosphere until they're fully grown, so they were only cut after that, in Gypsyworld, and put to use in countless other ways. And, of course, for every tree they cut, they planted one or more soon afterward.

The trees were to be marked with Day-Glo orange cords, tied around their trunks, and the six of them split up in pairs to do the work, once Cisco had explained how they would know which ones to choose. He also pointed out that since they would be working on a hillside, everyone could keep from getting lost by following the trees they'd marked back down again. The pairs, almost predictably, were formed by D insisting he "got" C, and A inviting E—which left the other two. Sometimes, not too often, everything works out perfectly, like that.

But, as soon as they were out of earshot of the others, Brenda started in.

"Look," she said to him, "we're overdue to have a little tell-the-truth time, don't you think? What the heck is going on, here?"

"Going on?" said Cisco. He'd gotten an expression on his face that managed to combine sweet innocence and total puzzlement. You'd think she'd asked him to describe the major differences between an evening dress designed in Paris in the early 1980s, and one from Tokyo, today. But yet, behind that look, there also seemed to be a twinkle in his eye.

She would have liked to shake him. That was *one* thing that she would have liked to do to him, *with* him— whatever.

"How, *going on?*" he said, again. The twinkle had evolved into a full-fledged smile.

Brenda stamped her foot, and hurt it just a little. That helped to keep her lips in line.

"You damn well know *exactly* what I mean," she said. "You aren't any accidental tourist, here. You think that I'd forgotten seeing you downtown and asking you for help? And watching you jump on that bus and run away? How come you did that, anyway? And, even more—how come you happen to be way out here, in the middle of this forest, just at the very moment that we come along? *I* say there's something fishy going on. And now I want to hear what *you* say."

Good Lord, she thought, I'm sounding like my mother talking to my father.

"Well," he said, "the nothing-but-the-truth is that my bus *did* come along. And I was late, already. Which meant I *had to* catch it. That's like a law of nature, *n'est-ce pas?* When *your* bus comes along, you better catch it."

Brenda looked severe. She also looked away to keep from smiling. Where did he get off, flashing French at *her?*

"I'm thinking of another law of nature," she opined, "that goes like this: When a fellow human begs for help, you give it to them."

She watched him wrap his arms around a tree trunk, and then tie the orange cord that he'd been holding. She thought he looked adept, experienced, at wrapping-arms-around. Which didn't mean he shouldn't keep on practicing, improving his technique.

"I know," he said. He looked contrite. "Good grief. Don't you think I felt like ca-ca, running off like that? Running out on such a person as yourself? You bet I did. And that's the reason, or a part of it, at least, that we're both here, right now."

"Say—*what?*" said Brenda. "*Your* feeling bad is why *I'm* standing in this trackless wilderness, having this peculiar conversation?"

"Yeah, uh-huh," said Cisco, nodding. "It sure is." He didn't look like someone having a bad time—no, quite the contrary.

She watched him making up his mind about . . . what he'd say next, she guessed. He tossed his head this way and that, and made some gestures with his hands; his lips were kind of moving, but not forming any words.

At last, he got it all together. "Yeah, all right," he said.

"The truth is that I lied, before, about the bracelets. I knew exactly who you were, the minute that I saw you, downtown; those bracelets *are* a label, sort of. Part of me—my feet, I guess—didn't want to get involved with you (you being from outside of Gypsyworld, and all), but other parts of me"—he touched his heart, and grinned—"sure did. You being *clearly* such a poor, pathetic, *needy* individual."

"I *see*," said Brenda, starting to smile back at him. "Poor, pathetic, needy . . ."

"Yes," said Cisco. "Notice I did not say 'gorgeous.' Absolutely not. And 'smart' and 'charming' never were a part of the attraction, either."

"And now?" said Brenda. "Now that we have known each other four whole days . . ."

"Now," he said, "upon mature *reflection,* with my contact lenses in, and after having spent four days in close *propinquity* . . ."

"All *right,*" said Brenda, doing Carrie's wave. "And me, I will admit the reason—or *a* reason—I asked *you* for help was that you looked to be the sort of person I might *relish* being helped by." She looked away and dropped her eyes, as she said that, giving him an opportunity to both absorb the compliment and, well, appreciate her profile.

"Okay, the *reason,*" Cisco said, "that both of us are here, right now, is I . . . discovered Josip and Marina thought it might be good to get you out of town. Not just you, the bunch of you. They didn't like the way the people in the town had been . . . reacting to your presence."

"Present company included," Brenda felt she should remind him, just a *little* meanly.

"They thought it would be best," said Cisco, totally ignoring that, "for you to learn the ways of Gypsyworld without receiving bad vibrations from the local populace. Who were being awfully blind and narrow minded, one might say."

"Yes, you sure *were,* weren't you?" said Brenda, pointedly, again—but looking like a grudge-free zone, she thought— she *hoped.* "But, tell me, how did *you* re-surface in our lives? How come we came together, here?"

Cisco shook his head and started striding up the slope. Brenda took a look and saw the tree that he was heading for. She followed in his footsteps, more or less, admiring the spring in his long legs, his sturdy boots, and other sights available to someone walking after someone else.

"I'd think it would be obvious," came floating back to her. "Josip and Marina worked that out with me. Together, we decided that they'd drive you out of town and drop you off . . . well, where they did. And that I, and Duffy, Babylon and Jackie would be where *we* were. We followed you all day, and then camped near you, overnight."

"You mean," said Brenda, in amazement, "that what you're telling me is this whole deal is something that the King and Queen *set up?*"

She was glad that Cisco couldn't see her face, just then. If he was telling her the truth—and she had every reason to believe he was—some most amazing things had taken place. All good, all positive, and unbeknownst to her, or any of the other kids. And of course there was one *other* thing, quite unbeknownst to *him,* that now was looking even less . . . applaudable than it had looked, before.

It seemed that he was saying, first of all, that Josip and Marina had decided they were going to let them go back home. That was first, and *most* amazing. And, apparently, they'd worked out a plan to make that happen. They were going to drive the kids to such-and-such a spot and drop them off (perhaps with a crude map, who knows?). Then, Cisco, here, would "come along" and "find them," sort of just by accident, and guide them to the border. They must have come to the conclusion, Brenda thought, that bringing them to Gypsyworld had been—as it turned out—a big mistake.

The second most amazing fact was Josip must have caused the Winnebago to break down (or stall, or stop—whatever) at that predetermined spot. In a sense, the King and Queen had *let* themselves be kidnapped! They'd realized (as soon as Dennis rattled off the kids' demands) that, even kidnapped, they could do exactly as they'd planned. The method would be slightly different; the result would be the same. They'd also seen that if they'd tried to tell the kids that they had planned to let them go, no one would have bought it. No, once that knife came out, the best thing they could do was play along, and that was what they'd done; Marina'd even gotten them to take some food along.

"They really did arrange it all," she said, in awestruck tones, this time.

"Well, yes," he said, and stopped and turned around to look at her. "You see, they *liked* you guys, Josip and Marina did. Of course,"—he dropped his eyes—"they needed my . . . cooperation—but that wasn't hard to get. And by the way, this really *is* the work I do. I just had to start out sooner than I'd planned."

Brenda's head was spinning, trying to sort things out. Cisco was being wonderful, she thought; he was telling her the truth. She really wished that she could do the same, try to make him see why they had done what they had done. And tell him she was sorry—that they *all* were, really.

But she didn't dare. It was better to say nothing, she believed; experience had taught her that. Let him go on thinking that they'd been "let off." Telling him what they had done would not do any good to anyone. Not to them (the five of them), nor to the other-them (the tiny possibility of him and her).

"I guess we're pretty lucky," she said, smiling at him, now. She felt a little bit ashamed, but also that she didn't have a choice. "Lucky all of you decided what you did. Although . . ." She paused, and then decided that she'd go ahead and press her luck. ". . . there's still the fact they brought us here to start with. And no one's ever told us why."

Cisco'd reached the big tree he'd been heading for, and now he leaned his back against it and looked down at her. Brenda didn't think that anyone had ever looked at her like that. She felt as if his eyes were going right into her heart, to see if it was tainted with dishonesty and faithlessness, or not. To see if he could really, truly, trust her.

She had to look away from him, again.

"I'm going to tell you," Cisco finally said. "I'll tell you why they brought you here—you ought to know—but first you'll have to promise me two things." He held two fingers up.

"The first one is"—he put one finger down—"that you agree to stay in Gypsyworld for six months more, starting from today."

Her eyes leaped up at him. She didn't know what-all was in her face, right then; it could have been a lot of things. In any case, *something* made him blush, and smile.

"I'd promise *you,* of course," he said, "that you'll be treated with so much respect and decency, you may doze off, from boredom." And he laughed. "After that time, we both should know if there'd be any point in having you stay longer. And, by way of an inducement, I should tell you: When we aren't in the field—that's doing work, my job— you'd keep on living with the King and Queen."

Brenda started to say something, but he hushed her.

"Wait," he said. "Just let me finish, first. The *second* promise is: You wouldn't tell the other kids about this conversation. Ever. You'll understand the reason why in just a minute, if you make those promises. Because *then* I'll tell you why they brought you here."

He held out a hand to her.

"So," he said, "is it a deal?"

"I don't know," she said. She nibbled at a thumbnail. "I guess I've got a few concerns, some questions in my mind." She also didn't want to seem too . . . easy. "One minor one would be: Suppose the King and Queen don't *want* me staying at their house, again?" She tried to make that casual, offhand.

"Don't worry," he replied. "If I asked them to, they'd let you, anyway." Now he looked a little bit uncertain.

"You see, it's my house, too," he said. "I'm Josip and Marina's son."

"You're *what?*" she almost shrieked. Was this her typical bad luck, that even crossed the border with her, into Gypsy-world? "Their *son?*"

"Ssh, yes," he said, "the only offspring of the King and Queen. But don't go thinking I'm a prince. Their offices are both elective."

"But maybe," Brenda babbled, "maybe *you'll* decide I shouldn't stay there." She hesitated, then. How could things get any worse? He was their son; she was their kidnapper. What were the chances *he* would ever fall in love with *her?*

"When you get to know me better," she went on, "and

learn more facts about my *past* and everything, maybe you won't want me with you any six months longer."

"Well," he said, "I doubt it, but let's see." He scratched his head, then raised the finger he'd been scratching with. He looked . . . undaunted, she would have to say.

"How about a First Amendment to the promises?" he asked. "If both parties freely make a speech and say so, you can leave and go back home before six months are up." He paused. "So, with that amendment"—his hand came out again—"is it a deal?"

Brenda tried to do a real quick job of adding all of the peculiar pluses in this deal to all of its strange minuses. If she could trust this boy, Francisco, she'd be risking, at the most, six months; if she couldn't trust him, who's to say that she was going to get out anyway? As far as Josip and Marina were concerned, *possibly* they'd put the blame for what had happened where a lot of it belonged, on Dennis.

On top of that, she *was* attracted to him, had been from the moment she'd laid eyes on him, and even up on top of *that* there was the possibility her folks had sold her to the King and Queen like so much sliced bologna. This could be the break she'd always longed for, her only chance to win the lottery of life. It could be the big brass ring, right there in front of her, before her eyes, but shaped like—*zut, alors!*—a human hand!

"Okay," she said, and shook with him. "I'll do it." She let out the breath that she'd been holding. "So, quick now, *tell* me!" She hadn't factored in her curiosity in reaching her decision, but now it just took over; she could barely wait. Why *had* they brought her here?

"Let's sit," said Cisco, and he looked around. There was a giant stump nearby. Duffy curled up by their feet—where both of them could reach him, if they wanted to.

"This is going to knock your socks off," he began. He spoke much softer then, and in a little while, he took her hand.

"Existing side by side," he said, "there are two worlds—the one that everyone calls Earth, and Gypsyworld. People who know how can travel back and forth between them. People from the Earth do not know how to do this; only gypsies do.

"The Earth and Gypsyworld are very different, at the present time. They are treated very differently by their respective populations. The people on the Earth are ruining their home. . . ."

As Brenda sat there listening, not knowing what to say (if anything), or even think (if anything), he told her why he thought that this was happening. He told her many of the people now on Earth still failed to notice they were part of a community of air, and soil, and water, and of plants and animals, and other people.

"They live," he said, "as if the only ones that matter are themselves. And so, their lifestyle may destroy them.

"As people, we in Gypsyworld are just like all of you. At some time, all of us—or, anyway, our ancestors—came here from Earth. The only way we're different is we have our own priorities and lifestyle."

He said that gypsies always paid attention to events on Earth. He explained that they had ways of getting back to Earth and watching people there and, yes, inviting some of them to come and move to Gypsyworld: the ones who seemed to have the same priorities and lifestyle *they* did. The ones they realized would make real fine gypsies, too.

But recently, an argument began to rage in Gypsyworld. It had been noticed that the situation on the Earth was getting worse, in large part just because (some gypsies claimed) the people lacked awareness. These gypsies thought the people on the Earth could still be *made* aware, and learn to live in harmony with air, and soil, and water, with plants and animals and other people.

"Those who took that point of view believed you didn't *have to* keep on doing what you're doing now," said Cisco. "They said it wasn't that you *must* destroy your precious home, and ultimately yourselves. These people thought that Earth could still be saved, by its own people, with our help.

"Still others here," he said, "believed we should do nothing. More people thought that way. They claimed that it's too late, and that it's hopeless. They also were afraid that dealings with the Earth might lead to Earth people finding out how they could cross the border into Gypsyworld, just on their own, and wreak some kind of havoc on this land, and on the people here. Earth people, as a group, just *cannot* change, these say. There's nothing positive that anyone can do for them.

"Josip and Marina disagree with that," said Cisco. "So, when they were elected King and Queen, they offered a proposal. They would make a trip to Earth and there collect five kids. Not necessarily the best kids they could find; in fact, they promised that a few of them would be . . . well, close to *rejects*—kids their parents didn't even want. These five kids would be a sample—like a test case—representative of all the kids and adults on the Earth. All the King and Queen would do would be to just expose those kids to how it is in Gypsyworld. Josip and Marina argued that they'd change, that they'd become like us, good friends of the environment. And if they did, that meant everyone on Earth *could* change, and we should help them, just as much as possible. We'd set up teaching programs, demonstration programs—bring Earth leaders here to see what we've accomplished. Make an all-out massive effort that, in time, would open everybody's eyes."

Brenda's eyes had gotten huge, as he told her that. He was right; her socks had been knocked off. To hear that she was in *another world* was sock-knocking enough. But then to hear that, in a way, the future of the Earth might very well depend on . . . *Alec, Carrie, Dennis* and *Elizabeth?* Too much! Oh, *much* too much. And she had promised that she wouldn't tell them what she knew (and how they had to act and all)! There were—there must be—half a million questions that she had to, ought to, ask, but Cisco kept on talking.

" . . . trouble was that though most gypsy people had agreed the King and Queen could go and get those kids from Earth, and run this small experiment, they started having second thoughts, as soon as Josip and Marina left. And by the time that they returned—with you five guys—a lot of folks had given way to panic. They were actually afraid that kids from Earth might *ruin* Gypsyworld, *infect* us, you could say, with Earthliness. With wastefulness, and harmfulness, and greed. Thank God, they said, that they'd insisted on those bracelets; at least they could identify the danger, right away."

Brenda'd started nodding. Everything was starting to make sense. All the little strange events, reactions, elements of gypsy life . . . why, seen from the perspective Cisco'd given her, all of these made sense. Gypsyworld *was* different from the Earth, and it was better. The way the gypsies lived, the things that they believed, even how they thought of kids and their intelligence—everything was better. Josip and Marina were about the nicest adults she'd ever known, and

Cisco . . . all *he* seemed to be was just the boy she'd always dreamed of!

But she had to interrupt him, now.

"Aren't we going to finish the experiment?" she asked. "I'll bet we'd change, if we were here a little longer. I *know* we would, in fact. Take me, I'm serious; I can tell I've changed already! And the other ones, Elizabeth . . ."

Cisco'd started doing head shakes, and he interrupted her, right back.

"I don't know," he said. "I'm not sure what's happening, exactly. The King and Queen were feeling pretty hopeless, when I spoke to them, before I came out here. They were afraid the people were so frightened and upset they'd closed their minds. You must remember"—and he shook his head, again—"we take good care of Gypsyworld, but we're still people just like you. We can get as weird and paranoid as anyone."

Brenda's head felt full of conflict and confusion. Poor Josip and Marina; *good* Josip and Marina. All they wanted was to help and save, and look how they got treated and resisted. And Cisco, here . . . he'd just let go her hand and now was holding her two shoulders, looking straight into her eyes, again!

"I don't think you had to change," he said. "I think you've always loved the beauty and the wonder of the Earth . . ."

Her hands were on his elbows, then; the breaths that they were taking mingled in the forest air. She couldn't wait. Before he got to it, she said it for him.

" . . . and certain other people," Brenda whispered, just before they kissed.

fifteen

❦

FOR ABOUT TWELVE HOURS after that first kiss, Brenda had as "nice" a day as anyone had ever wished her. Or, possibly, a good deal nicer.

The two of them had kept on marking trees till lunchtime, pausing now and then to nuzzle one another and rejoice about the prospect of a half year more of doing "work" like this.

At midday, and with all the marking that they'd planned to do completed, they then wrapped arms around each other's waists and started down the slope, with Duffy at their heels. Before they reached the campsite, Jackie suddenly appeared and landed on a limb in front of them, and cawed. That made them laugh and drop their arms and keep on going single file. Over lunch, they learned the other pairs had also finished with the areas they'd hoped to do.

"Excellent," said Cisco. "With you guys here, I'm more than three times faster than I would have been, alone. So, how about we make some miles, this afternoon? I'm sure you're anxious to start up, again."

"I'm not in any rush," Elizabeth replied to that. "We

thought marking trees was fun, right, Alec? We even found some blueberries."

"Oh, yeah?" said Dennis. "So, how come no one's passing them around? I thought we all were gonna get fair shares of everything to eat."

"We didn't have a thing to put them in," said Alec. "We were planning to go back this afternoon and pick a whole lot more—and maybe even have enough for pancakes and a pie." But seeing Carrie put a finger down her throat, he laughed and quickly added, "*Elizabeth* was going to do that, not Chef Boyardee, here. There's tons of them up there, just growing wild, I guess."

"We could pick some on our way," said Cisco. "I'm glad you noticed them." And Alec beamed with pride. "But not all of them are wild. That's what makes this an agroforest; it's got crops in it, as well as trees and wildlife. You'll see more of them, along the way we're going."

As they got their stuff together, Cisco told them how the rural parts of Gypsyworld were organized. People lived in villages, instead of being scattered far apart ("we're *very* sociable, we gypsies," with a little blink at Brenda), and managed the vast acreage around them.

"We try to make the best of everything that nature gives us," he explained. "And even do improvements on it— terraces on hillsides, stuff like that. In general, we plant our food crops in the better soils; grasslands are for useful grazing animals, and forests—well, you're seeing one. We're big on never wasting land, or hurting it. On Earth, a third of all the total land mass of the continents is shot, already. And more of it goes down the tubes, each year."

"Come *on*," said Carrie. "You're exaggerating, right? A *third* of all the land? I don't believe it."

"Yep, it's true," said Cisco. "Most of that is desert, the rest of it's been built on, or paved over. Every year, more topsoil's blown away, or washed away, or poisoned. Twenty-four-billion tons a year. It's hard to think, imagine, how much soil that is. And when it's gone, it's gone."

"*Right,*" said Dennis, unexpectedly. "That's what happened over there in Africa. That's why they have those famines, right?"

"Africa and other places," Cisco said. "Forty thousand babies die each day, all over Earth, basically because they can't get proper food and care."

"But aren't there too many people, anyway?" said Alec.

"Absolutely true," said Cisco. "And more 'too many' all the time. Here, people have one kid, or two—or maybe three, which often is an accident. On Earth, you're going to add another ninety million, probably, next year—that's even *after* fifteen million babies die."

"Yikes," said Alec. "Ninety *million?*" He had a piece of twig and he was scratching numbers on the ground, doing long division, it appeared.

"About," said Cisco.

"Let's see," said Alec. And he checked his figures. "Yes! You were saying how you couldn't think of how much topsoil twenty-four-billion tons would be? Well, if every one of those ninety million people weighed two hundred and sixty-six pounds—if you could imagine *that*—their combined weight would be just about twenty-four-billion tons. Which I guess'd be land you couldn't grow food on to feed those ninety million extra people."

"Scary, isn't it?" said Cisco.

◆　◆　◆

While that talk was going on, Brenda tried to look from kid to kid and guess what everyone was thinking. It was hard to say.

Clearly, all of them had heard environmental facts before, on Earth Day, or in school, or on TV, most likely. Dennis knew that they'd had famines over there in Africa, but even she, a black American, did not identify that much with kids in Ethiopia, or Chad, or the Sudan. It had said on television that one trouble with those countries was that people over there kept messing up their land by overgrazing it, and that instead of cutting down their herds and planting grains to eat, they simply kept on doing what they'd always done, for generations. She had to wonder: Were those people stubborn, or just dumb?

Now that she'd come to think of it, however, she could see that people in America who kept on sending all that junk from cars and factories and power plants into the atmosphere were doing just the same as those old Sudanese. They were threatening their own existence, sure as anything. So—were *they,* like, stubborn, or just dumb? Like the gypsies wondered, would they, could they, change *their* lifestyle? Or would they keep on putting off and putting off, and doing further studies?

She wondered whether she, herself, would ever have considered doing anything that might be inconvenient or expensive or just *hard,* if she had not (let's face it) fallen (gulp!) in love with Cisco.

Or, put it this way: Lacking Cisco, would the "love" she had for other kids (say, Alec, Carrie, Dennis and Elizabeth), or for her parents or her unborn children, or five billion strangers all around the world—would *that* love motivate a person such as her enough to cause her to cut back on something that she liked, or liked to do?

She looked at Alec, Carrie, Dennis and Elizabeth again and tried to read their minds. How selfish, lazy, stubborn, dumb, shortsighted or plain self-destructive were they?

She really didn't know—at all. It was funny; there in Gypsyworld out in the woods they seemed okay, or better than okay, together. Maybe that was just because they wanted to get out, however; all of them except Elizabeth, perhaps—and maybe Alec, it was hard to tell. And Dennis really did look up to Cisco, you could see that, all the time, the way he followed him around. Carrie? It was hard to know what Carrie really wanted. In many ways, she seemed the toughest of them all to read; she seemed so inconsistent. When she could do her music, she was like a different person—gentle, easygoing, satisfied. Cisco'd made a little flutelike instrument, just out of bark and wood, and it was neat to hear what she got out of it. Everybody loved the pure, high melodies she played. It was as if she breathed in forest air, and blew, and turned it into music.

◆ ◆ ◆

They did pick berries on the way, and after that they really pushed it. Cisco said there was this lake he'd like to camp beside, that night. One of its feeder streams was great for fishing, and he said he'd catch them trout for supper. He said the lake was very beautiful, and that he thought they'd love it there as much as he did. Brenda felt that he was saying that to her, especially—that he was looking forward to her seeing . . . well, another of his loves, a place that she had things in common with.

Hiking, Brenda felt that she was in a private little atmosphere (so different from her first day in the woods). It was a zone of rosy-colored, slightly scented air that moved along as slowly or as fast as she did. In it, she felt light and energetic;

on rough terrain, she seemed to know exactly where to step, she bounded up the hills and then flowed down their sides. She hardly talked at all, and she could see, for once, most all the things that Cisco pointed out to them.

This, she thought, is what it's like to be in love. The *real, real* thing. The difference is the confidence you feel. In him, in you, in your ability to deal with any situation that comes up. Before, when she had *thought* she was in love with someone, there were always certain ogres lurking in the shadows on the edge of the relationship: the great What Ifs. "What If he decides to . . . ?" "What If I don't . . . ?" "What If we just aren't . . . ?" With Cisco, she felt no What Ifs. She was sure of him and of herself, and that seemed odd, seeing that they'd known each other hardly any time at all. She knew they still had lots to learn about each other, and she refused to put him on a pedestal—pretend that he was perfect. But she was sure that there'd be nothing forced, or rushed, or frantic in the way their love expressed itself; agreements would evolve, she thought, and never be demanded.

From time to time, she walked beside him, on a deer track, and when she did, she'd turn her head from time to time and look at him. *He's real, all right,* she'd think, *and so am I. So, here we go!* she'd think, and smile, inside her perfect little atmosphere.

◆　◆　◆

The lake was all that Cisco'd said it was. In shape, it was a kind of crescent moon, so though it was a mile and some from tip to tip, a person in a boat, or swimming, wouldn't ever be too far from shore. He'd said that it was very deep out in the middle and didn't have a lot of vegetation growing in it; that made the water very clear. The woods around it were a mix: white birches and white pine. They found a perfect campsite near the bottom of the crescent; there even was a fairly sandy beach, nearby.

Elizabeth began her preparations for a pie at once—by asking Alec if he'd go and wash the berries. She was afraid the pie would not come out right; she was going to have to use a lot of strange (to her) equipment: a reflector oven Cisco had, a flashlight for a rolling pin. She asked them all if they were sure they didn't want to eat the berries plain, before she ruined them.

Carrie said, "I think you ought to try, Elizabeth. No one'll blame you if it doesn't come out great. And if it does, you'll be a local hero. You'd never guess it, looking at my dainty figure"—she spun around for them, her head thrown back, one hand behind her neck—"but I just *dote* on baked goods." And she giggled.

"Yeah," said Dennis. "I could use a slab of pie, myself. And, hey, I'd stick around and help, except I made a bet with Cisco. I said that I'd be able to call turkeys—and get answers, too, I mean—before we got up to the border. So I have to practice every chance I have." He looked at Cisco. "That's providing I can use your caller, man."

"Help yourself," said Cisco. "You know where it lives. Me, I'm going to give ol' Babylon a little treat, and then start hauling in those trout—I hope. If Elizabeth and I get lucky, we'll have a pie *and* brain-food supper."

Dennis said that *he'd* give Babylon her treat—a carrot and some oats—before he started calling turkeys, and so Cisco got his rod and reel, his haversack, and the little folding shovel, and headed troutward through the trees. Carrie said she'd gather wood and start the fire, but that then she absolutely had to have a bath and wash her hair. Although she didn't think that it was going to rain, Brenda made a little lean-to they could use in case it did, out of plastic tarps. After that, she rigged the food packs so that she could pull them up and off the ground, secure from porcupines, et cetera, that night. She decided she'd go in the water, too, when Carrie did.

They walked, together, down the shore to where the fairly sandy beach was, and they undressed, together, underneath the pines. The water in the lake was pretty frigid; even Brenda, veteran of morning dips in mountain streams, agreed that that was so—but only after she had gasped for breath the first time she dunked into it. They both shampooed their hair, and Brenda felt a sense of comradeship with Carrie that reminded her of back at Josip and Marina's house, but even better. It seemed to her they'd gotten down to basics, this time—that in addition to their clothes they'd shed their differences, and now were just two women, sharing, being natural in natural surroundings.

By the time they got back to the campsite, Elizabeth was rolling out her pie crust, looking flushed and stressed, while Alec tried to tell her everything was going great. Carrie told Elizabeth that, much as she liked pie, she *really* didn't care if it was edible, or not.

"I appreciate that you were nice enough to try to make a treat for us," she said. "I really do." And Brenda saw that when Elizabeth looked up at her, the two of them *both* blushed, before they smiled.

"I think I'll go and see how Cisco's doing," Brenda said to everyone in general. And then, to Carrie, "Want to come?"

Carrie dropped her eyes and started saying, "No, no, that's all right . . . ," but Brenda said, "Come *on*. We'll have to go as quiet as two mouses, so's not to scare the fish; it should be fun. And I really want to see just how you fish for trout, don't you?"

So, Carrie said if Brenda was *completely* sure it was all right, she'd love to go, and the two of them took off in the direction Cisco'd headed, stepping very carefully, trying not to make a sound.

When, at last, they saw him, he was sitting on a rock right on the lakeshore, and he wasn't fishing anymore. He *had* been fishing, though; they could see he'd had good luck. His catch, already cleaned, was lying on another rock beside him, covered with wet ferns. He was holding something up quite near one ear; it had to be—it was!—a little radio.

Brenda looked at Carrie with her eyebrows raised. She hadn't known that Cisco had a radio. He'd never mentioned one, or used one in her sight. Now, he thumbed the little wheel set in its side and jammed its small antenna down; he'd finished listening. He put the radio inside his haversack and stood. It seemed that he was ready to return to camp.

Brenda tapped on Carrie's shoulder, put a finger to her lips, and jerked her head in the direction they had come from. Then, staying doubled over, she began to scurry through the pines, away from there. When they were surely out of sight and sound, she said to Carrie she'd felt guilty, spying on him there, like that. She said that she was sure he had good reasons for not telling them he had a radio. Carrie pursed her lips and nodded. Brenda wasn't sure just what she was agreeing with.

◆ ◆ ◆

Cisco was quiet during dinner. Brenda wondered if the other people noticed; she sure did. He fried the trout—and they were perfect—looking grim. The pie (its crust was under-done and didn't hold together all that well) was definitely edible, although Elizabeth was far from satisfied. She said she *had* to make another one for them—somehow, some-where, sometime—she wanted them to have the best pie in the world. Cisco didn't offer any reassurances; he didn't tell her, sure, of course she could and would. And while the washing up was going on, he kept sitting by the fire, staring into it.

When all the pans and dishes had been put away, and all the food suspended from the trees, he told them he had something that he wished to say to them. Dennis, Alec and Elizabeth, suspecting nothing, smiled as they came over and sat down; Dennis had been showing them how great he was at skipping stones. Carrie was outwardly relaxed, at least; Brenda hugged her knees.

Cisco cleared his throat.

"I have some news that's not so hot," he said. Brenda took a breath and held it. "I got it off this radio I have; I was listening to it while I was fishing." He kept on looking at the fire, not at them.

"When you took the King and Queen out of their house"—he paused—"at *knifepoint,* someone saw you. It was the neighbors' little girl; she's only four years old, and she was looking out the window of her room . . ." His voice was flat, expressionless; it was not a friendly, caring sound. Brenda let the breath out.

At first, he said, the neighbors didn't pay attention to the child; she was the sort who liked to make up stories, totally outlandish ones. But when the Winnebago never did come back that night, and the little girl kept on insisting she was telling them the truth, the neighbors gave the cops a call, the first thing in the morning. When they came out, that afternoon, they opened up the unlocked door of Josip and Marina's house and went inside to look around. Of course they saw the unwashed breakfast dishes, sitting on the table. They knew that wasn't like the King and Queen, both of whom were well-known neat freaks.

While the two policemen were still there, continued Cisco, who should pull right in the little drive but Josip and Marina in the Winnebago. Questioned by the cops, they told the truth, of course—and the rope burns on their wrists and ankles offered further evidence. But, unsurprisingly, they stuck up for the kids as well, and said that people shouldn't heap a lot of blame on them—that all they wanted was to get back home, as soon as possible.

"They insisted you were real good kids," said Cisco. His voice was still quite calm and uninflected, but Brenda wondered if she also heard a little irony or bitterness in there. "And they said they hoped you'd make it out of Gypsyworld, and that would be the end of it."

The other gypsies, though (said Cisco), were of quite a different mind. The members of the Gypsyworld Assembly were pretty angry. They saw this knifepoint business as a serious offense, as "proof" of what those kids were like. They felt that they were different, dangerous people—"bad." They believed that if the kids *were* able to discover how to make it out of Gypsyworld, they also possibly might understand the gypsies' secret ways of getting in.

"A consensus finally was reached," said Cisco. "They want to capture you and bring you back. They think of you as criminals."

There was a silence, broken by Elizabeth.

"Josip and Marina, then—they're fine?" she asked.

Cisco nodded. "Yes, completely. From what I understand, they hid a little ways away—once they had escaped from you—and waited till you left the van. Then they got the extra key—they keep one, taped, behind the dashboard—switched over to the extra tank of ethanol, and drove back home."

"What?" said Dennis. "Ethanol? What's that? You mean we weren't out of gas?"

"It's a kind of alcohol," said Cisco. "We make it from wood—from trees like those you marked. It burns much cleaner than your gasoline. Oh, no, you weren't out of fuel." He said all that as if his mind was somewhere else.

Alec, sitting tailor fashion on the ground, had started picking at the bottom of one trouser leg. He didn't look at Cisco.

"You mentioned other people, the Assembly, but, well, *you* are a gypsy, also," he said, slowly. "You're probably quite angry at us, too. I could hardly blame you." He switched his nervous picking to his sock. "Have you decided what you're going to do with us?"

Up to that point, Brenda'd sat there like a stone, and she'd been *feeling* like a stone as well—desensitized, just there, a block of nothingness. Now she began to add things up, put together all the facts she had.

Cisco now had heard their guilty secret, that they'd held his parents captive and had threatened one of them, at least, his *mother*, with that lousy knife. He knew that *she'd* been part of doing that (and, of course, had never told him).

But, so far, he hadn't told the other four *his* secrets: that Josip and Marina were his parents, and that all of them were there to (maybe) show the gypsies that they ought to help to save the Earth.

What did that mean? she wondered. Was it possible he wasn't going to tie them up and take them back to town? Might he decide to keep on going with them, keep the whole experiment alive, even though he hated all their guts?

"I am angry," Cisco said. "You lied to me when we first met, and never changed your story after we were getting to be friends." Brenda squeezed her eyes tight shut. "And now I don't know what to do; I feel I'm in a trap. On the one hand, I believe the King and Queen *would* like it if I got you to the border, as I told you that I would. But most other gypsies want you captured and I know that, now; they've sent some people after you. As a citizen, I should do what the other people want." He paused and shook his head. "I just don't understand. You've told me that the King and Queen were good to you. You could easily have hurt someone, real badly—one of them. What was the rush, for heaven's sake?" He rubbed a hand across his mouth. "Yes, sure I'm angry. Disappointed, too." Now he sounded bitter, and he sounded mad.

Brenda opened up her eyes and raised her head and looked at all of them. Cisco was back to staring at the fire. All the rest of them were looking at the ground. Everything seemed totally unfair, to her.

"Well, you shouldn't feel that way about Elizabeth," she said. This was something she could do at least, one tiny bit of fairness. "She spoke up against our doing what we did. She would've stopped us if she could've."

"That's right," said Alec, instantly. "I had to talk her into it; I wanted her to stay with . . . all the rest of us. She didn't have a thing to do with the idea."

"It's my fault more than anyone," said Carrie. "I could have kept it all from happening; I know I could've. But I didn't. I encouraged it. Looking back, it seems like a mistake, and now I'm sorry." She said that straight at Cisco. "But at the time . . ." She shrugged and seemed to pull some walls back up, around herself.

"Well, I'm the one responsible," said Dennis. This was even worse than screwing up at home. At home, they always told him what he'd done, *accused* him of it, and then, after that, they told him what he'd *get,* for punishment. This time, he had to, like, accuse *himself.* "It was my idea, and I'm the one who had the knife, an' everything. I don't think that I'd have hurt the King and Queen, no matter what they did." He scratched his head. "But the truth is, I don't know, I guess. Things happen that a person doesn't *mean,* some-times." Brenda thought his voice was hoarser than she'd ever heard it, and she noticed that he couldn't bring himself to look at Cisco.

Elizabeth said, "Cisco," and she looked at him, and waited till he looked at her. "No one's told you something that you ought to know. We aren't who we said we are. Student-council members and all that. All of us were either bought or taken—kidnapped—by the King and Queen. They told us that. So what we did to them was pretty much the same as what they did to some of us, except they didn't use a knife. They brought us here to Gypsyworld against our wishes, and they never told us why. That wasn't right of *them,* I think. It's true I liked it here as much or more than home, but that's beside the point. I got to know the King and Queen. But I also got to know these other kids. And now I like them all, no matter what they may have done." She smiled. "And definitely you, as well; we all like you very much, I think. We were wrong in doing what we did. But they were also wrong to take us. I don't excuse us, but there is that explanation. You should know that. I hate your being angry at us."

Brenda shook her head, amazed. Elizabeth, as usual, was clear about her feelings, and only she, of all the other four, remembered Cisco didn't know how they had gotten there. Or so she thought. There was lots, however, that *Elizabeth* still didn't know. Only she and Cisco knew it all, and now he was upset with them and furious at her. Dennis may have been the one that held the knife against his mother's throat, but it was she who'd kicked him in the heart.

While she was thinking that, he was kind of gulping and then saying to Elizabeth that he was glad she'd spoken up, and that he understood what they had done a little better, now. That he could see how this would look to them. He sighed, and shook his head, and said, "Not meaning it as an excuse . . . ," that gypsies, after all, were people, too. He said he needed to "digest all this, awhile," that he was feeling overwhelmed and "well, uncertain about *lots* of things." He said he didn't want to talk about it anymore, right then.

He stood up, after saying that, and went and got his toothbrush and then headed for the lakeshore, never looking once toward Brenda. She slowly got up, too, picked up her sleeping bag, and walked a good ways from the fire. Her fear of darkness and wild animals never crossed her mind. The only thing she felt was that her life was, finally, ruined.

sixteen

BRENDA PUT HER HEAD INSIDE her sleeping bag that night, and pulled her knees up to her chest, and bawled. The feeling she had had all day, while hiking to the lake, that *confidence,* had been exposed for what it was: a fake, a fraud, a masterpiece of self-delusion. Her thing with Cisco was no different (she saw now) than other things she'd had with half a dozen other boys. No one told the whole, entire truth to anyone; people kept a few cards up their sleeves, and skeletons in closets. But hers had been exposed and, naturally, despised. No one would ever love her just the way she was, which meant no one would ever really love her. Everyone would find a reason to despise her, if they knew her long enough.

And she, she'd simply have to stop imagining that *someone else* was all that wonderful. Boys had their good sides and their usefulness, but they could not be counted on to understand, to always be there when you needed them. It—reality—was more the way her mother'd put it to her, once: "A woman's like a jockey, more'n anything. She gets the best horse that she can, and then she learns just how to ride him, how to keep him running straight. That means sugar cubes sometimes, but sometimes it's the whip. He don't want to run straight every day, but she can make him. One way or another, she had better be the boss. And if she's any good, he'll never know it."

Brenda cried some more, when she thought that. She didn't *want* the world to be the way her mother thought it was.

She didn't fall asleep till sometime after midnight, and when she woke up, at a quarter after six, she saw that there was movement down there near the fireplace, where the other ones had spent the night. Cisco was fully dressed and walking back and forth. He had a piece of paper in his hand that he was looking at. Carrie'd gotten out of bed, and she was pulling on her pants. Elizabeth and Alec, both, were still inside their sleeping bags, but sitting up. There wasn't any sign of Dennis.

Brenda slid out of her bag and pulled her high-tops on; she hadn't bothered to undress at all, the night before. She started walking toward the others. Carrie saw her coming, came to meet her.

"Dennis split, again," she whispered, when they'd gotten close. "Sometime in the night; no one heard him go. He took his sleeping bag and everything, and left a note right next to me. He put my flashlight on it."

"What'd it say?" said Brenda. She was curious, and cared, but not a lot, not yet. Mostly, she felt kind of numb.

"I don't know," said Carrie. Now she was sounding real excited—worried, too. "It was folded over. On the outside, it said, 'Carrie, please give this to Cisco.' So I did. He was dressed already, and just sitting by the fire. But it was weird. He hadn't even noticed Dennis wasn't there. He didn't notice that until I pointed to the place his sleeping bag had been and handed him the note. But I'll bet he's read it twenty times, by now."

Brenda walked back to the fireplace, with Carrie. All four kids just looked at Cisco; Elizabeth and Alec sitting, the other girls still standing. He finally dropped the hand that held the note down by his side, and raised his eyes and looked around, and saw that everyone was staring at him.

"All right," he told them. "This is what it says." He got the note chest high again, and read from it.

" 'Dear Cisco. I hope you'll take the others to the border. The one the gypsies want to catch and persecute'—he probably meant 'prosecute'—'is me. The others didn't do no harm. They'll be better off without me, just in case the gypsies catch you all. I'm sorry for the stuff I did, for doing that to Josip and Marina. And thanks for trying to teach me outdoors stuff. You teach real good. Take it easy. Dennis.' "

When he was finished reading, everyone kept staring at him. He dropped the hand that held the note down by his side. No one knew what he was thinking; what, if anything, he had decided, overnight.

At last he took a big deep breath and looked at all of them. Brenda got the feeling he was *counting,* too, making sure the rest of them were there, still there. When he looked at her, he didn't look her in the eye.

"This is not . . . acceptable," he finally said. He lifted up the note and struck it with the back of his left hand. "I made him do this, by that attitude of mine. So, now I have to find him, bring him back with us. We're all in this together, like a family. Dennis mustn't blame himself for being Dennis. The truth is that I care about him, very much." His voice was hollow. Brenda thought he sounded whipped, much the way that she'd been feeling.

He looked around the group again, more slowly. Not hatefully, at all. Closer to lovingly; *acceptingly,* for sure.

Brenda nodded her agreement with the things he'd said, and looked down at the ground. Dennis *had* been being Dennis, or anyway, what he thought Dennis ought to be. He was not a bad kid, not at all. He'd followed Cisco like his second puppy dog, every chance he got. And he'd carried more than his fair share, ever since they'd left the Winnebago. She'd seen how much he wanted their approval, and their friendship—Carrie's in particular. Now was the time for them to show him that they cared. It was interesting, she thought: the King and Queen had been the first to call them "family"; it had seemed ridiculous, back then. Now, here was Cisco doing it, who really *was* their son. A weird coincidence, for sure. And now, the usage didn't seem so strange.

When she looked up, she saw that Alec and Elizabeth had gotten out of their sleeping bags, and both of them were dressing, hastily. But not—she knew, could tell this just from watching them—not because they were embarrassed to be seen half naked. They were simply hurrying.

"We're going with you." It was Carrie who expressed what all of them were thinking. "It's up to all of us to show him what we feel about him."

Cisco bit his lower lip, but then he nodded.

"Yes. Okay," he said. "He'll start out fast, but . . . well, he's not a woodsman, yet. Duffy may not be a bloodhound, but he's good at finding strays." He led the dog to where the boy had had his sleeping bag and pointed at the ground. He put his finger right down on the spot.

"*Dennis,* Duff," he said. "*Find Dennis.*"

The dog kept sniffing at the place that Cisco pointed to.

He'd lift his nose a second, and then put it right back down again. It really seemed that he was trying to memorize the smell, fix it firmly in his mind.

Meanwhile, Brenda ran back to the spot she'd left her sleeping bag, and rolled it up, and got it in her pack along with other items Alec brought her. When they straightened up from doing that, Carrie handed each of them a Carrie Breakfast Special: one chocolate bar, resting on a piece of pie. Brenda saw Elizabeth had gotten two more of the same, for Cisco and herself.

◆　◆　◆

They started, following the dog, who led, with Cisco right behind him. Even Babylon, for once, seemed energetic and cooperative, a member of the team. Jackie kept pace easily, floating tree to tree. Not often, but from time to time, Cisco pointed out a footprint or a broken twig, a clump of grass pressed down—some sign that told him Dennis was ahead of them, and they were on his trail. There was very little talking, but the four of them all looked real hard. Cisco'd taught them that already: if you want to see things in the woods, you have to pay attention, look around. Their heads went left and right and up and down. You'd think that we were windup dolls, or tourists, like, at Disneyworld, thought Brenda.

They hiked four hours without stopping once. Some people in the group were more than ready for a rest: Carrie, Alec, Brenda, to name three. But none of them was going to ask for one. Cisco, up ahead with Duff, would be the one to make decisions. He'd say when they would stop, or eat; if he'd started trotting, they'd have tried to, too.

Then, suddenly, he *did* stop. The others were around him

in a minute, looking at the same thing he was looking at, a river, the biggest one they'd seen in Gypsyworld. The lake they'd camped beside had not been that much wider than that river was, in places. But, while the lake was deep, and flat, the river had some boulders sticking out of it, and you could see the bottom, quite a ways from shore. And it was moving.

"This is the Lavengro," Cisco said. "It's our most major river. Let's take ten minutes' rest, and have a little lunch." He smiled and shook his head. "Dennis must have hated running into this. I bet he had a hard time making up his mind which way to go."

"How come?" said Alec. "What difference would it make?"

"It could make lots," said Cisco. "We talked about that, he and I. How it was best to go *down*stream, if you were lost or needed help, but *up* if what you wanted was to get across. I don't suppose he'd think that we'd be coming after him."

While he was saying that, he'd opened up the donkey's two saddlebags. Carrie helped him get out cheese and biscuits and some raisiny granola kind of stuff; it was just a snack that they were going to have, apparently. Carrie also found the bag of crystals they could mix with water, to make an orange drink. Dennis, he had liked that orange drink, a lot.

Duffy'd started to his left, upstream, but he'd returned when he saw everyone was sitting down. Cisco broke off bits of biscuit for him. Carrie came back from the river's edge, holding a canteen.

"Is this okay to drink?" She shook the thing at Cisco. "It sure is nice and cool. No garbage in it, either—as far as I could see."

"Yeah," he said. "It's drinkable." He smiled. "Of course it is."

"Excuse *me,*" Carrie said. "I forgot I was in *Gypsyworld.*" But she was smiling, too.

Babylon, meanwhile, had wandered to her left, and disappeared into the trees. No one gave that any thought. The donkey would often take a little stroll all by herself, go foraging. Now, presumably, she'd gone to get a drink, as well.

But, hardly half a minute later, she began to "sing" (as Cisco called those sounds she sometimes made)—though *shriek* and *bellow* were the words that came to Brenda's mind. In any case, her *ee-ee-yaws* began and didn't stop. To everyone but Cisco, she sounded angry, or in pain.

"Babby *wants* something," he said, getting to his feet. "I'll go and see." He started off, in the direction of the sound.

Elizabeth got up and followed him; the crow was sitting on her shoulder. The other three came quickly after.

Upstream from where they'd stopped to eat, the river took a big bend to the left, and what the mule had done, by cutting through the trees, was come out on the other side of that big bend. So, she could see a stretch of river that they couldn't see, from where they'd had their snack.

The river looked about the same; it was almost every bit as wide, for sure. The major difference was—and this is what the donkey was looking at, and bawling at, from right down by the water's edge—that clinging to a boulder, way out there near midstream, was a soaked, bedraggled boy.

Babby'd found her buddy Dennis, sure enough.

seventeen

"GOOD GRIEF!" said Cisco. "Crazy little stinker. He must've tried to cross it."

He was yanking off his shirt, as he said that. There wasn't any hesitation on his part. What he planned to do was very clear to everyone on shore, and must have even been to Dennis, clinging to that slick, black rock.

"Hang on, amigo!" Cisco shouted, anyway. "Gonna get you offa there, no problem. Everything's okay now, buddy."

Brenda watched him pull his trousers off. Everything was *not* okay, she thought, not even close. The boy was out there in the current, *had been* out there for God only knows how long. His lower half was in the water, still, and she had *drunk* a little of that water not too long before, and thought how nice and cool it was. If he was reached in time, the boy would be a dead weight, coming back, half again as heavy with his sodden clothes on, still. You couldn't very well undress him, out there on that rock.

Cisco, in his black-and-white-striped briefs, was fishing in a saddlebag. The other kids were frozen, looking back and forth between the boy and him. Brenda'd seen all three of them in swimming; they were much, much worse than

Cisco, who wasn't any ace. All of them could stay afloat, and maybe do a lap or two (she thought) if they were in a heated pool, with no one making waves. But as far as being any help in getting someone off a rock in the middle of a swiftly moving, ice-cold river . . . well, forget it.

"Ah," said Cisco, pulling out a modest coil of rope.

Carrie, now, was right down at the water's edge. "Hold on, Dennis!" she was hollering. "Cisco's going to get you off. We came to look for you. We need you back with us. You hold on tight for just a little longer!"

Dennis didn't lift his head, or wave, or give the slightest sign that he had heard what she had said. But at least he did appear to keep on holding tight.

"Maybe, if I get out there with this, and you guys hold the other end . . ." Cisco was talking softly, almost to himself. He uncoiled a little rope. "Except it isn't near as long . . ." He shook his head and coiled it up again, slipped it over his left shoulder. "I *told* my mom that I'd regret it if I didn't take that lifeguard job."

Almost before she knew what she was doing, Brenda'd pushed her pants down and stepped out of them; she was wearing a bright turquoise string bikini. And then—and close to angrily—she pulled off her shoes and socks. One moment she'd been staring at the boy out there, and the next one she was doing that. What had happened was that, suddenly, she'd felt what he was feeling, clinging to that rock. She *knew* what helplessness was all about; she understood *alone*. He needed her to save him. And she was going to do that, just because. She almost wished that Cisco wasn't into it, already; this didn't have a thing to do with her and Cisco. Except that she suspected she could use his help.

"I'm going, too," she said to him, unnecessarily, not even looking at him. She hesitated, left her turquoise tank top on; she couldn't have said why, exactly. "I took a class once. I'm a real good swimmer—as I guess you know." She started moving toward the river. The second part of what she said was true—and she'd *watched* a class in lifesaving, down at the Y, one time.

She picked up Cisco's trousers, on the way.

"I'll make some water wings for him," she added. She emptied all the pockets and began to tie knots in the pants legs, as she waded in. She didn't look, but she could hear that he was coming, wading after her.

The water, it was cold all right, but not that bad (she told herself). It was too deep for her to run in, but she hurried through it, pumping with her arms; she felt like someone in a walking race. Soon, it was waist deep, and slowly getting deeper, still.

She saw they ought to head upstream a little farther. Once they started swimming, they'd go downstream faster than across (she thought); the current was that strong. She veered and kept on wading, fast as possible, leaning up against the moving river. It was best to keep in contact with the bottom for as long as possible. She thought that Dennis must have found a log, or branch, to hold on to, that he'd used some *something* as a kind of surfboard. Probably he'd hit the rock and lost it—and his sleeping bag, and just about his life. Behind her, she could hear that Carrie, Alec and Elizabeth were now all yelling toward the boy.

"We *love* you!" she heard Carrie shout. "You just hold on. They'll be there in a minute."

Brenda kept an eye on Dennis as she waded. She was sure his hands and feet were numb. His cheek was flat against the rock, but he was watching them. His bright, black eyes were way wide open; he looked terrified and desperate.

She turned to Cisco, who'd stayed close behind her. "Maybe we ought to tie ourselves together, now," she said. "And, look, let's tie these water wings between us."

She trapped some air inside the knotted pants legs, and used the middle of the rope to tie the waistband shut. The water wings looked half inflated, droopy. The ones made by the class she'd watched had looked much better. The current pushed against her body. A few more steps and she'd be forced to swim. She and Cisco got the rope ends tied around their waists.

"Ready?" she asked Cisco. "I think if we aim straight across, the current ought to take us to him. So—okay?"

He nodded. "Yes. He's looking . . . yeah, let's go."

Brenda bent her knees and drove straight forward, leveled out, and started swimming hard. She was glad they didn't have too far to go, that they'd been able to keep wading such a long way out. But now, the river's strength was scary, and the water sure was cold. When she lifted up her head to breathe, she saw that Cisco wasn't doing quite as well as she was, swimming. But he was certainly all right, and stroking strongly with his arms, especially. He kept his head and shoulders out of water, as he swam; his swimming style was not Olympic quality.

"Here we come, amigo!" Cisco hollered to the boy, now bobbing up and down with every stroke he took. Brenda'd started treading water; she'd swum far enough to let the river carry her. She could steer herself directly to the rock. Cisco had to swim, still, but he would also make it to the boy, all right. It looked as if Step One would be accomplished.

When Brenda floated up and put her hands on Dennis, she was shocked. He felt ice cold and rigid. She slid up on the rock and clutched him, put her chest right on his back, hoping that her body heat would warm him up a little.

"You okay?" she said to him. Her lips brushed up against his neck, beside his ear.

"Cold," he croaked, hoarser than she'd ever heard him. She could see his lips were sort of purple. "An'—an' I can't move my fingers none."

Just then, Cisco reached them, coming swiftly in the current, totally in its control. He got a grip on Dennis's right leg, cried "Whoops!" and very nearly pulled the two of them clear off the rock, before he let the leg go, grabbed the rock, instead. He pulled himself around behind it, where the river pushed him up against the other two. Panting, he got half on top of Brenda. They lay there for a moment, like a sloppy triple-decker sandwich.

"Look," Brenda said to Cisco, "Dennis can't hold on to anything; his hands are cold. So what we're going to have to do is this. You slide under me and get ahold of him. The way we're going to leave this rock is me first, then the two of you, together."

She was saying stuff as quickly as she thought of it. The main thing was to have a plan and do it, quickly. Cisco wasn't any expert in the water; it was up to her to tell him what was what, to be the boss.

"You'll be on your back," she told him, "holding Dennis on your chest. I'm gonna tow you, but you gotta help. You gotta push hard off the rock, and then keep kicking with your legs, you understand? If we can get you on top of those water wings, you'll float a whole lot better, so we'll try to do that in a minute, pull them into place."

Cisco nodded; he seemed to see what she was driving at. He moved his body slightly, and she got her weight onto a knee, and he slid off her and then under her, on top of Dennis. She could then maneuver the inflated pants legs in between herself and Cisco, and he got them underneath his armpits.

"Good," he said. The boy let out a little grunt, perhaps to show that he was with it, perhaps because of all that weight on him.

"Now, Dennis." Brenda raised her voice. She wanted to be sure she had the boy's attention; they needed his cooperation. "When we tell you to, you gotta just let go the rock, you understand? *Cisco's* got ahold of you, and he'll be swimming on his back, and *he* won't let you go, no matter what; you'll be right on top of him. We're going to be all right. It's almost over now. You understand me, what you gotta do?"

As she yelled all that, Brenda wasn't sure at all that they would be all right. She didn't know if what she'd planned would work or not. But it was based on these realities: Dennis couldn't help himself, Cisco had the strongest arms, and she could swim by far the best. And she also knew that if they stayed in that cold water too much longer, none of them would make it to the shore alive. It *was* "almost over now," one way or another.

She got her toes against the rock. She planned to do a shallow dive, shoot herself toward shore.

"Ready for the next step, Cisco? You got your arm around him tight?" Cisco nodded.

"Okay, Dennis!" Brenda shouted at the boy. "You let go the rock. You hear me, now? Let go the goddamn rock! I know your fingers aren't working right, but you can pull your arms back toward your chest—so do it!"

For the next few seconds, the expression "death grip" filled her mind. She imagined she and Cisco trying to pry this little sucker's hands up, somehow—and maybe hitting him upside his head a time or two, so that he didn't grab back hold, again. But then she saw his fingers sliding back, just resting clawlike on the rock, now. The boy had put his life in Cisco's hands.

"Okay," she said—to Cisco, now. "Can you pull him over on your chest, on top of you? Just roll right over on the rock?" He could and did. "That's good. Now slide down—here, I'll help you—so we get you into place to push off hard against the current, right? We'll both go on 'three.' I'll dive against the current and start swimming; you push off and then keep kicking. Ready?" She was pretty sure she saw him nod. He was on his back, his right arm locked around the boy, across his chest. Dennis had his eyes closed; his face had now become serene and childlike. "One, two, *three*!"

Arms outstretched, head down between them, Brenda fired out. She started stroking, almost right away, hoping to hold on to her momentum, angling toward shore. But after half a dozen strokes, the rope around her waist went taut and almost stopped her cold. She dug in, kicking hard and grabbing water with her hands; they still were moving shoreward, sure enough—as well as starting to drift down. She kept her face down in the water till she *had to* breathe. But having gulped some air (she took it on the downstream side), she closed her eyes again and just swam hard. She never dared to look around, the times she had to breathe; if they'd been swept around the bend, she didn't want to know it. She felt that she was dragging . . . oh, an ocean liner.

Then, all at once, the weight behind her was immovable. She was stroking, but still staying in one place, not moving anymore. And then she felt hands on her shoulders, and she stopped the flailing of her arms and looked up into Alec's geeky face. Being tallest, he had waded farthest out. Behind him, she saw Carrie and Elizabeth; both of them were shouting, laughing, cheering, jumping up and down and slapping at the water. Like Alec, they were fully dressed.

She turned her head and there was Cisco, standing just a little ways behind her, holding Dennis up with both arms now, one around his body, one under his knees. Dennis had his head on Cisco's shoulder, and his eyes were open. Back on shore, the donkey was braying and the dog was barking, and the crow was circling around. Everyone was safe, and they were back together.

My family, thought Brenda, more satisfied than she had been in her entire life. She smiled. You're doing it again, she thought. But, for the moment, anyway, she didn't care.

eighteen

NOT FAR FROM where they'd come ashore, there was a
wooded area that had large boulders on the river side of it, a
line of rocks, some of them as big as hippos lying down, that
must have been pushed up there by the river, years before,
during some spring flood. Elizabeth and Alec built a long
hot fire up against the largest of them, so that its heat would
be reflected back, and Carrie got a clothesline strung, and
they and everybody else took off whatever they were wearing
and then wrapped themselves in unzipped sleeping bags,
and blankets.

Dennis needed help. His hands and feet were still not
working right. Cisco had to carry him up there, and hold
him off the ground while Carrie peeled his clothes off. After
he'd been dried and wrapped up warmly, the two of them
kept working on his circulation: rubbing, rubbing, rubbing. It was a painful process for him, getting warm, but
gradually it happened, and he tried to smile and joke and
make the best of it. But Brenda saw that he was hurting.
And embarrassed, and exhausted. She and everybody else
refrained from asking questions.

For everyone but him, the fire soon was mostly useful as a

dryer for their clothes. The air was much, much warmer than the water, and people started moving here and there, setting up the campsite. Everybody smiled at everybody else, a lot. Brenda thought they looked like primitives, barefoot with these heavy cloaks wrapped tight around them. Now and then, a cloak would fall off, too—anytime a person tried to use both hands for something—and depending on the individual, and the importance of the thing that he or she was doing, it just might lie there on the ground until the task was done. Alec and Elizabeth, still the shyest of the group, blushed and giggled once or twice, but Brenda thought that even they were cool, compared to how the kids she knew back home would be. It seemed these latest happenings had put things even more completely in perspective, making clear the differences between the things that mattered and the trivial. And, for the moment anyway, the thing that mattered most was that the six of them were safe and back together. What anybody wore, or didn't wear, was altogether incidental.

Brenda and Elizabeth prepared the goulash that they had for dinner. With the help of Cisco's seasonings, it tasted *something* like the one they'd had their first night at the King and Queen's. While making it, they talked about how long ago that seemed, and how much everyone had changed. They decided dinner ought to be at four p.m., that night; most of them were starving—what with that "lunch" they'd had, or didn't have—and lots of them were interested in early bedtimes.

By the time the goulash "reached its flavor peak," as Brenda said, their clothes were fully dry, so they could switch to "formal dress" (in Carrie's words) for dinner. Eating, everyone relaxed and started talking, almost dreamily, about their feelings, and the day and, finally, the future.

"Now, it seems so *stupid,* even saying this," said Dennis, "but what I thought was, deep down, you all *wanted* me to split. That everyone'd say 'good riddance.' " He put down the bowl that he'd been eating from and pulled his blanket tight around his shoulders. Even with his clothes on, he was not quite warm enough.

"Oh, Dennis," Carrie said. "You are such a *jerk.* No one was blaming you. If Josip and Marina had just driven us back home, you'd have been a *hero.*" And she wrinkled up her nose at him.

"What I'd like to know," said Alec, "is how on earth you got out where you were. *I'm* a rotten swimmer, but you—I didn't know that you could swim at all." Alec thought that seeing as Dennis started this, it'd be all right for him to . . . show an interest.

"I can't," said Dennis. "But what I did—there were these *branches,* all along the shore. I tied—oh, three of them, I think it was—together, with the clothesline that we'd saved. That way, I had a kind of raft to float my pack across on. The thing is, at first I thought that it was shallow all the way across. And when I found out different, well, I thought that I could sort of half lie on my raft and *kick* across the deepest part. What I didn't know about was *currents,* man." He shook his head. "But *now* I do, all right."

"That must have been so *scary,*" said Elizabeth. "To suddenly start *shooting* down the river."

"Tell me about it," Dennis said, but softly, with his eyes half closed. "When I hit the rock and got knocked off my raft, I thought for sure that I'd be drownded. I don't remember getting up there on that rock at all." He was almost whispering. "But I sure remember *being* there." He was looking at the ground.

Carrie shifted to her right, so she was sitting touching

him. She put her hand on his near shoulder, and her voice was gentler than they'd ever heard it.

"Don't think about that, now," she said. "It's over. It's like a bad dream, total history."

"No," he said. "There's stuff in there I wanta keep remembering forever." He picked his head up then, and looked at all the others. *"No one's* ever cared for me, or helped me, like the bunch of you just did. I almost can't believe it, even now. But I want you to know this. I'd give my *life* for any of you, now, and that's no bull, I swear it." His voice cracked, as he finished saying that, and Carrie put her hand on his bowed head, and ruffled up his hair, as he croaked out, "I'm sorry."

"Nothing to be sorry over," Cisco said. That came out extra loud; he looked surprised and cleared his throat, and got the volume down. "I guess we all feel pretty much like that about each other; what I think it is, is wonderful. And we are so damn *lucky,* too. To have a—what's her name? the great, great swimming champ of yours? Janet Evans, is it? Who could have known we'd have a *Janet Evans* with us?" He looked at Brenda, smiled, and shook his head. With wonder on his face, this time.

"Yeah, yeah, *right,"* she said. "Don't kid yourself. I was trying to stay warm, is all."

That wasn't the first time Cisco'd said a special thing to her. When they'd got back to the shore, and he had carried Dennis up onto the bank and put him down, he'd turned to her at once and softly said, "Thank God for you. You saved our lives. You're wonderful."

She'd had to shake her head at that, and say, "I needed *you,* to do it." But in one sense it was true; she probably *had* saved their lives. Cisco would have gone ahead and tried to save the boy without her, but it was possible—or even probable—he wouldn't have been able to get back to shore with him. If he'd been alone, the current surely would have taken them around the bend.

What she wasn't sure of was the present state of their relationship, in either of their minds. They certainly were friends again—but *kissing* kind of friends? *Six-months-staying* kind of friends? She didn't know. He'd gotten mad and "disappointed" (as he'd said). At her, *with* her, as well as all the others. Had that feeling gone away? Or had it just been painted over by these new developments?

And, how about her own desires? Was she ready to feel tight with him, again? In *love* with him, again? He'd hurt her pretty badly, too. *Gratitude* was not the basis for a love relationship, she didn't think. She wasn't sure exactly *what* she wanted, at this point.

"Just out of curiosity," said Alec, "how far up the river *do* you have to go before it's possible to wade across?" Sometimes, Alec's endless questions came in handy, Brenda thought.

"Quite a ways," said Cisco, turning toward him. "Five-six miles, I'd guess. You'll see. That's the way that we'll be going next—upstream. If we went about that far the other way, we'd come to Gypsyworld's main power plant. This river here provides a big part of our electricity."

"Huh," said Alec. "Interesting." He grinned, and had a twinkle in his eye (thought Brenda). "A nice, clean, non-polluting power source, of course. But where's the nuclear facility you haven't mentioned yet?"

"*Nowhere*—are you nuts?" said Cisco, and he grimaced. But then he grinned, himself. "You're kidding, aren't you? Good grief, *of course* you are. But since you asked so nicely,

I'll just tell you almost all the rest—meaning, of our electricity—it comes from wind and those collecting cells you've seen on people's houses. Photovoltaics is the name for that. It's a system that converts the radiation from the sun directly into electricity. *That's* going to be the biggie in the future, here."

"Yeah, but," Carrie said, "if you *also* could keep *Alec* living here, you'd have a constant hot-air source, as well. I bet you probably could run another hundred windmills on . . . hey, Alec, cut it out!" He once again had risen to attack her, and as ineffectively as ever. This time he'd tried to use his sleeping bag to smother her. She snatched it from his hands and sat on it, and he retreated to his place again, while looking rather pleased by his audacity.

Practical Elizabeth veered onto something else. "I'm wondering: what's next?" she said to Cisco. "I mean, it's great you're going to help us, but *can* we—even with your help—avoid those people that are searching for us? Can't they sort of block the routes we'd have to take, to make it to the border?"

Alec, nodding by her side, agreed. "Good point," he said.

"Well, one thing on our side," said Cisco, "is they're not aware I'm with you. They think that you're just by yourselves, and know you're not familiar with the territory. I imagine they'll be guessing you'll stay near the road, that you won't like the forest."

Brenda's eyes got wider, hearing that. If Cisco knew the gypsies *didn't* know that he was with them, that meant Josip and Marina hadn't told them what their plans had been. How they had planned to rendezvous with Cisco, more or less, and let him be the one to show the five the ways of

Gypsyworld. In other words, his *parents*, Josip and Marina, kept some secrets from some people, too. It was getting clear to her that gypsies, even good ones like the King and Queen, could be as devious and sly as anyone. And try to . . . well, excuse the bad things that they did by saying that they had good reasons.

"So, what you're saying is that we can go some way they'd never think we would or could," said Alec.

"Yes, exactly right," said Cisco. "I can put myself in gypsies' shoes—figure where they'd go if they were smart (and they *are* smart), where they'd try to catch you. Then we can go another way, and leave them empty-handed."

"Yeah, but," Carrie said, "it sounds as if the route we'd have to take would be a whole lot longer. And take us quite a bit more time." She didn't sound enthusiastic.

"Uh-huh," said Cisco, nodding slowly, with a little smile. "You student-council types would get to see a lot of rural Gypsyworld, all right. Any problems with that?"

Carrie milked the moment, holding center stage; she knew all eyes were on her. She frowned down at the ground and licked her lips, as if about to speak. She picked her head up and checked out the others, one by one. Everyone looked grim, even apprehensive.

So then she winked and quickly said, "Hell, no! You want to know the truth? I'm not in any hurry to go *anywhere*, right now. Now that I've got my little sweetie back!"

And, with that, she grabbed ahold of Dennis, pulled him hard against her side, and kissed him on the cheek. Everybody laughed, including him, and almost everyone (including her) then asked themselves (but not out loud) if she was serious, or not.

Alec, looking at Elizabeth beside him, saw this demonstration as a positive development—someone showing feelings for another person. He'd never done that in his life, if you didn't count his mother, in the days when he was still a little kid.

"How about supplies?" Elizabeth now had to know. "When we run out of what we've got, what then? It won't be all that long. D'you see us living off the land?"

Brenda winced inside, when she heard that. *Living* off the *land?* she thought. There's trouble.

Of course sometimes you read that in the paper: how so-and-so survived on "nuts and berries" after getting lost in such-and-such a "trackless wilderness." But that was not for her, she didn't think. She'd rather put spare time and extra energy in things like *kissing* (maybe), rather than in trying to scrounge up *food*. Good relationships within the group, she feared, would not go hand in hand with "living off the land."

"We *could* do that, I guess," said Cisco, "but I'm thinking that might take a lot of time"—(smart boy, thought Brenda)—"we'd rather use in other ways." (Possibly a genius, even.)

"What I'm hoping we can do," he said, "is sneak into a village, maybe more than one, and get . . . well, resupplied by people I know pretty well, people who are friends of mine, and of my . . . gracious majesties, the King and Queen."

Brenda gaped at him and had to work to keep from giggling. She was pretty sure he'd *almost* said "my parents," that he'd barely caught himself before he spilled some pretty spicy beans. Now, he refused to meet the look that she was giving him; his eyes went everywhere, except in her direction.

That made her wish she could have made some little calming, soothing gesture at that point, that she could have let him know that she was *sympathizing* with his need to keep some *secrets* from the others. She wished she could have patted him, twice, sweetly, on the knee. And left him wondering (along with her) exactly what she'd meant by that.

She was also wondering another thing: what their "gracious majesties," the King and Queen, were up to now. Might they be able to find ways, back in the capital, to help the fugitives some more?

nineteen

"WE BEEN THINKING," Josip said. "Thinking and investigating. Looking into this and that." He flicked a finger, back and forth, between the Queen's chair and his own. "Marina and myself, the two of us together. And, as a consequence, we have a little something . . ." For him, he sounded nervous and uncertain.

"Is along the lines of a *suggestion*," said Marina, diplomatically. "With, as well, what might be called a *proposition*, down there in the middle, like a juicy plum. We thought that maybe you would offer, possibly, a *taste* of these, to the Assembly."

There were three other people in their living room, all former royalty themselves, and every one a present member of that same august Assembly. And each an old friend of the King and Queen.

Anwar was tall and slender, silver haired and elegant. He always wore a flower—and it had to be a blue one—in his jacket's buttonhole. "Is such a hopeful color, blue," he often said. People thought he hoped to be elected King again, someday, and also live forever.

Finita was, perhaps, the strongest woman in the world.

Give her a place to stand, and she could lift an ox right off the ground. She had a little lisping voice that sounded like a five-year-old's, and a friendly, cheerful disposition. If she had been aggressive and the sort to hold a grudge, she might have been elected Queen a lot of times.

Carlo was a very average-looking man of medium height and build with black hair and a black mustache, and he could play the balalaika. Almost everybody had a relative who looked and sounded much like Carlo—which was why he got elected King, one time, but never would be reelected.

"I volunteer to thtick my thumb in your suggestion," said Finita, and she held that digit up, and giggled. "There'th nothing I like more than wipe, wed plumth." Her thumb looked long and strong enough to pull a cantaloupe from the LaBrea tar pits.

"Before we get to that," Marina said, while smiling at her friend, "a bit of background. Something that we think we know."

"Is concerning those five kids," put in her husband.

"Hey," said Carlo, "everybody knows *one* thing concerning those five kids. We're gonna apprehend them 'momentarily'—by that I mean the *searchers* will. Was on the radio, this morning."

"I know," said Josip. "Exact same 'momentarily' as yesterday, and day before. No, no, my friends. The thing we think we know is that it's not so easy to find a little group of small-to-midsize kids in many, many miles of agroforest. Lotsa places kids can hide, out there."

"True, true," said elegant Anwar, stroking his lean jawline. "And dragnets always have some holes, correct? Is in the *definition* of the word, if I am not mistaken."

"Exactly so. Which makes us think the place to try and capture them would be the *border,*" said Marina. "That is our suggestion—that we concentrate our efforts on the border. The fact is, we believe we know exactly where they'll try to cross. Has been *revealed* to us."

Anwar, Carlo and Finita looked at one another. Being gypsies, they believed in revelations and in special powers. Indeed, in Gypsyworld, a host of studies had been undertaken, *scientific* studies into the effectiveness of pendulums, divining rods, and other tools and forms of what is known as ESP in other places.

Josip and Marina had been tested and accredited by experts at the GSF, the Gypsyworld Science Foundation. It had been established that, without real effort on their parts (*trying,* funnily enough, reduced these powers drastically), they often "learned" some things that later on came true. For old times' sake, they kept that crystal ball, there on a table in their living room, but nobody had ever seen them use it.

"As you know," said Josip, "we are sympathetic to those kids. We believe that they are good. We wish that we'd been able to proceed with our experiment. Good grief, if only people had cooperated here, those children might have changed . . ."

". . . and shown us that the Earth, with help from all of us, could still be saved," Marina added. "We think the saving of the Earth to be a project people would enjoy."

"Never mind all that," said Carlo, sounding like her slightly older cousin, "give us some specifics. What you want from us?"

"We want your help in selling our idea to the Assembly," said Josip. "And this is the idea . . ." He gestured toward his wife.

"A group of us will travel to the border, to the place that we've been . . . shown," Marina said. "This group, beside yourselves, to be *our*selves and half a dozen members of Assembly who are *most un*sympathetic to the kids, and to the whole experiment that we proposed. We'll set up what I think is called a *stakeout,* there. Some word of that sort."

"Of course," said Josip, "other sections of the border should be covered, too. Is always possible that we are wrong, although"—he winked and smiled—"I absolutely doubt it."

"Jutht a minute, here," Finita said. "I get confuthed. I thought you hoped the kidth would make it thafely home."

"Well, in a way we do," replied Marina, smoothly. "But at the same time we are law-abiding thitizens—uh, *cit*izens—of Gypsyworld. The Assembly has ruled the children should be captured and brought back. It is our duty to . . . cooperate, I think." She dropped her eyes and tried to look obedient.

Anwar smoothed his silver hair.

"We know each other for a long, long time," he said. "If I understand you right, you want us to convince Assembly to make this ambush at the border. You allege that this will make it *possible,* at least, for them to seize the children. You are convinced these kids will not be captured by the searchers, but will show up at the spot that's been revealed to you."

Josip nodded to all that.

"But, my old friends," continued Anwar, "there is more to this than that, not so? When we first begin discussions, you maintained you had a *proposition,* like a juicy plum, that went with the suggestion for the ambush. I suspect"—he smiled an elegant and understanding smile—"we haven't heard that proposition, yet."

"Exactly right!" cried Josip, cheerfully, "so, here's the deal . . ."

◆　◆　◆

After their guests had left, Josip looked across the room at his beloved wife and blew her one enthusiastic kiss.

"I'm feeling pretty sure they bought it," he opined. "And I think that they'll succeed in selling it, as well."

"You're such a brilliant trader," said Marina. "In the old days, you'd have had a *herd* of horses. And you always *are* an optimist about your deals. But I agree; I think you're right. You made the sort of proposition that a gypsy has to fall in love with. Tricky, but completely fair." She shook her head, admiringly, and smiled.

"Now all we have to hope," he said, "is Cisco gets them past the searchers, to the border. And that he chooses where we said he would, to cross."

"Sure he can, and will," Marina said. "Even if he falls in love along the way—as I've been having feelings that he might—he'll have his wits about him. That boy's his father's son, you know." And, laughing, she got up and crossed the room, and sat down in her husband's lap.

"Hoping so, for sure," he said, and wrapped his arms around her.

twenty

❧

THE GOULASH and a good eleven-hour sleep were
all that Dennis needed to recover. He and everybody else got
up at dawn, and all of them were on the move by sunrise.
This was to be their first day, traveling, as fugitives—
knowing there were other people in the woods who "wanted"
them.

Before they'd gone five miles upstream, they found a
decent place to cross the river. Up where they were, the
great Lavengro's width and depth were cut in half from
where they'd been, and its current wasn't any threat at all,
unless you were an insect on a leaf. No one had to swim
a stroke, except for Duff, and he enjoyed the water, anytime.

In fact, as soon as he saw people taking off their shoes and
socks, he jumped right in and swam across, and then right
back again—perhaps to show how easily a dog could con-
quer such a mighty river. But only after he had made the
trip a third and final time did Duffy shake himself. And
then not carelessly, it seemed. He walked around and chose a
spot quite close to Jackie, who was picking at the gravel on
the shoreline. And she, instead of flying off or screaming

when the shower hit, just bobbed her head a time or two and preened her feathers with her active beak.

"Wait. Was that on purpose?" Brenda asked. She had watched this whole performance from the start. "Did Duffy *mean* to shake himself on her?"

"You'd have to ask him, to be sure," said Cisco. "But me, I've seen the same routine before. They do a lot of stuff together. Sometimes he gives her rides, right on his back."

"You're kidding me." She looked at him, suspiciously.

"Absolutely not," he said, and made an X right on the pocket of his work shirt. "They cost her half a cookie, though."

"Now I know you're kidding me," she said.

But at lunch that day she made a point of giving Jackie one of her Fig Newtons, and she kept an eye on her till it was gone.

"Jackie ate it all," she said to Cisco, as their caravan resumed its progress through the trees. "All of my Fig Newton. She didn't hide it, and she didn't share it with McDuff and get a ride. She just ate it all."

"Of course," he answered smoothly. "Duffy doesn't like the little seeds in Newtons. But try her with a homemade chocolate chip sometime."

"There aren't any," Brenda said. "We've only got the one kind left."

"Oh, that's a shame," said Cisco. "And who knows when we'll have a chance to bake some more. Just promise me you'll stick around until we do, all right? I really, really hope you'll see the famous riding crow."

"Yeah, sure," said Brenda, laughing. He sounded perfectly sincere, she thought, but that was such a . . . silly thing to say. "And also till I see the multiplying mule, I'll bet, and other equally amazing animals." She could play that kind of game.

"Exactly. Like the rueful crawling man, for instance," Cisco said. "The one who wonders if you can forgive him." Suddenly, his voice had gone dead serious.

He'd stopped, and she came up to him and stopped beside him.

"I don't want to see that one," she said. "Of course I can. Forgive you. And I think I have. I understand your being so upset. I was just afraid. Of screwing everything completely up."

She made a fist and touched him on the arm with it. He, in turn, reached out and took her other hand; now they were facing one another.

It was quiet in the woods, too quiet. Cisco looked around. It wasn't only Babylon and Duffy that he didn't hear; everyone had stopped. The donkey, the dog, and all four kids were staring at the two of them. Brenda, turning too, decided that they looked like people just before their favorite TV soap began—happily expectant. *Too* expectant, Brenda thought; Carrie wore a grin from here to there.

Just then, Jackie started cawing in the distance. Either Jackie or another crow, but everyone reacted, just the same. People knelt or squatted by the nearest tree; Babylon and Duffy both lay down, at Cisco's signal. The cawing stopped and then began again, but from a greater distance—phew. It was Jackie, almost certainly. She was Cisco's early warning system, and she cawed at strangers, first from one side of the place they were and then the other. About two minutes later, she'd repeat the same routine. In that way, Cisco'd learn if they, the other group, was moving or had stopped. But anytime a stranger crow cawed anywhere near them, Jackie would fly straight and fast and silently to Cisco, showing him it wasn't she who'd called.

They waited and heard other calls, gradually more distant. Whoever Jackie'd seen was angling away from them. Cisco straightened up.

"There's a gravel road up there," he said. "It seems as if they're on it, whoever they are. Let's get going. We can cross behind them."

Carrie, standing, put her grin back on.

"I'm not in any rush," she said. "If you two want to go ahead and finish . . ." And she made a little circle motion with her hand, while aiming rapid nods at Brenda.

She, however, wasn't ready, yet, to kid around with this relationship. She'd spent the minutes while the crow held everyone's attention trying to adjust to what he'd said, and how she'd answered him, and where that left . . . things. She could feel her heartbeat, still. She supposed that they were back to where they'd been before, but somehow it—or she—felt different. Not worse or better, necessarily—just different.

She made a little gesture, Carrie's gesture, back at Carrie and the others. Cisco didn't try to take her hand again. And when they started up, she paused so she could walk alone.

After about a quarter of an hour, Carrie made a point of catching up to her.

"Look, I'm sorry," she began. "I didn't think . . ."

"I know," said Brenda, and she turned and smiled at her. "It's just confusing, still. There's so much going on, and everything. I knew you weren't being mean."

"*Good,*" said Carrie. " 'Cause I really want to get to be your friend."

"You are already," Brenda said. "As far as I'm concerned. Things seem to happen fast and fabulous, in Gypsyworld."

With that, they put their arms around each other's shoulders, so that they walked in step, together, for a little way.

Behind them, Alec said, "Amazing," to himself. It made him think—he *told* himself—that maybe *anything* could happen.

◆ ◆ ◆

When they'd stopped to eat, that noon, Cisco'd drawn a little map to show the rest of them the way he planned to get from where they were to where he hoped to be some five days later. There was a certain spot he had in mind, right near the border. His route was all cross-country, full of loops and turns. It would bring them near two villages, one that very evening, and the next (he called them, simply, Village One and Village Two) in two or three days' time. Both of them had people living in them who were friends of his, and who would give or sell him some supplies.

"This first place," he explained, "has all the houses close together—so everyone can stretch his nose from one end of the village to the other. I wouldn't think of taking this whole mob in there, at any time. Even by myself, I'm going to wait until it's dark, and park old Babylon—my shopping cart—just out of town, back in the forest, still."

"I don't get it," Alec said. "No one's after *you*. Why can't you march right in and pick up anything you want?"

"Oh, I maybe could," said Cisco. He seemed careful not to look at Brenda. "But the less attention I attract, the better. You see, I shouldn't even be up here, right now, based on where I started out. And I shouldn't need supplies so soon. Also, I'd prefer it if I didn't have to answer any questions. We gypsies, we have lots of curiosity—suspicions, too, sometimes." He paused. "For no good reason, whatsoever." Brenda thought he might be overdoing it.

"How about the second village, then?" Elizabeth inquired. "Are you going to take us into Village Two?"

"Is there a mall in that one?" Dennis asked. "That's what she *really* wants to know. Me, too. I want to get a sweetheart ring, for Carrie." He made a comic face, and Carrie said, "Oh, sure. I *bet* you do, big spender. U-W-F-M. Using what for money?"

"No, really," said Elizabeth. "I think I'd love to see a village here in Gypsyworld. A *country* village, how it is, and all." She looked at Dennis. "I don't want to shop. I haven't any money, either."

"We'll see. I know I'd like to take you in there," Cisco said. "Maybe even spend the night. I have some very special friends there, older people, Marius and Katya. I got Babylon from them. They're livestock breeders, among other things; Babylon could stay in their corral, and nobody would notice. Their place is on the edge of town, and I'm sure they'd understand your . . . situation. They're pretty independent thinkers."

"They sound great," said Brenda. "I love the *names* in Gypsyworld."

"Marius and Katya are *big* names," Cisco said. "Just about the biggest in the country. They were King and Queen ten times, the most that anyone has ever been. The last time, they both said 'enough'; they'll never serve again. But they're still Gypsyworld's first family."

"They must be sort of like the Kennedys, back home," said Carrie. "Being all that famous."

"Or George and Martha Washington, maybe," Alec said. "Except he only wanted to be President two times."

"I guess," said Cisco, vaguely. "It's hard to imagine anyone as popular as Marius and Katya. Or, I don't know, as *versatile*. Besides their breeding farm, and being rulers, they've started up and managed major companies—all sorts of different things."

"Wow!" Elizabeth exclaimed. "They sure *do* sound historical."

"They sound like *millionaires,*" said Dennis. "Every big shot is, I don't care where you are."

"Well—you'll see," said Cisco. "Maybe."

"I sure hope so," Carrie said. "I could go for a nice hot bath and fluffy towels, one time."

◆ ◆ ◆

It rained that afternoon, and it was raining, still, that evening, at the time that Cisco, leading Babylon, prepared to leave for Village One.

"Gee," said Carrie, from the shelter of the cozy lean-to that they'd made. "I'm so *sorry* that I can't go with you, Cisc. But you won't forget my Whopper, will you? With large fries? And try to hurry back, okay? They're much less tasty, cold."

"Anything from Taco Bell is fine with me," said Dennis.

"And chocolate chips, for cookies." That was Brenda.

"I can't understand a word you're saying, little glutton couch bananas," Cisco answered. And giving them his space-commander-on-a-dangerous-mission wave, he led the donkey off, through the rain.

He didn't make it back till after midnight, and he hadn't gotten chocolate chips, a Whopper, or a single thing from Taco Bell. But at least the rain had stopped, and when he slid into his sleeping bag—someone had left it neatly opened, at the far end of the lean-to—Brenda raised her head and whispered, "Welcome home." That might have brought him happy dreams—and even made it *slightly* easier for him to struggle to his feet a little after dawn, as usual, about four hours later.

◆ ◆ ◆

For the next two days, they roamed through parts of Gypsyworld that seemed, in terms of looks, as close as you could come to postcard perfect. The weather was ideal, after the rain; any leaf the sun hit seemed to dance and glisten, and the air was so completely clear that every hilltop seemed to offer them (in Carrie's words) "a totally Top Forty view."

And there were many hilltops on their route. The better roads, in general, were in the valleys, which meant that they climbed hills, some of them quite steep. But gypsy foresters had terraced many of these slopes, so that the soil, instead of washing down and off them (to be lost in streams and rivers and the sea), was held and planted with a wide variety of crops and shrubs and trees. Cisco explained how all the different plants they saw were used for different purposes— some for food or fodder, some to fortify the soil, and even some that could be used in fuel production, making ethanol. He told them how the plant biologists in Gypsyworld were using and *creating* an enormous range of plant varieties, some of them undreamed of, yet, on Earth.

"Plants are the key to everyone's survival," he insisted. This was on the second day. They were sitting on a wooded hillside, by a spring, and looking at a ridge now covered with young pines. Between the two hills was a narrow valley that would lead them to the settlement where Marius and Katya lived.

"I'm talking plants in croplands," he went on, "and plants in grasslands, plants in forests. All the plants are hard at work, even as we speak." He smiled. "Just think. They use the energy they get out of the sun to take some water and some CO_2 and a little other stuff, and combine them into carbohydrates—food for animals and people. *Photosynthesis,* that's called, in case you've never heard of it, amigos: the miracle, the process that makes healthy worlds and healthy people possible."

"And is even good to look at." Alec laughed as he said that. "Or at least the plants are. Compared to city streets, for instance. Or even shopping malls," he felt obliged to add.

"I agree with you, so there," said Carrie. She was serious. Brenda clapped her hands, but noiselessly; nobody noticed, even.

"At least I do right here, right now," continued Carrie. "Sitting here with you guys, being fugitives and all, and not having to . . . well, *deal with* all the *normal* crap in life. Like going to school, or planning a career, or trying to impress some guy—*you* know. For now, I just don't *need* what's on those streets, or in those malls."

"And when it comes to guys," said Dennis, "hey! *I'm* impressed, already. But, no kidding, I was thinking that same thing, last night. Even though we're, like, the object of a *manhunt,* I feel more relaxed and happier, right now, than when I'm doing something regular, at home. It's weird. The *atmosphere* is different, here in Gypsyworld." He laughed. "No smog."

"Listening to Cisco, what you come to think is: everyone has more or less the same priorities and lifestyle," Alec said. "And they're pretty simple. Just like our life right now is simple; there's no competition and we get along. I don't know, though." He shook his head.

"How d'you mean?" said Dennis.

"Well, for instance, I can't quite believe the *kids* here can be all that different—just for instance," Alec said. "In how they treat each other, stuff like that. What I'm saying is, someone like me, I never had real friends at home, and I doubt I'd have them here. You guys have all been really nice, but that's because of . . . circumstances."

"Yeah, *but,*" Brenda had to say, "it's *possible* the gypsy kids *are* different. Look at Cisco, though of course he's *slightly* older." She pointed and he covered up his face. "Their parents live so differently than ours do. Maybe, growing up somewhere like this, all of *us* would be real different, too."

"I'm sure *I* would be," said Elizabeth. "More relaxed." She touched Alec on the knee. "*You* would be, too; I'm sure of it. Here, all you'd have to be is good old basic Alec—sweet and smart and funny, and an artist. You wouldn't have to deal with people wanting you to be another way. Or be like anybody else."

Alec blinked and looked uncertain.

"Well, thanks," he finally said, "but I don't know." His voice was flat, impersonal, and he was staring to one side, away from everyone, just staring at the nearest stand of trees. "It's hard to imagine yourself being any different, really *being* different—no matter how the other people were." Finally, his head turned slowly, and he cleared his throat. "But, thanks, Elizabeth," he said to her, while *looking* at her, too. His voice had gotten softer. "What you said"—he looked down at the ground and started mumbling—"it-meant-a-lot-to-me."

No one filled the silence right away. Then:

"*Anything* is possible," said Dennis, firmly. "That first day, I thought that everybody in that van was hopeless, that I was with the biggest bunch of—I won't even *say* it—that

I'd ever met. Except"—he turned to Carrie—"I always thought that *you* were cute. And now—and it isn't just because you saved my life—it's totally the opposite." He smiled, but seemed a little . . . hesitant, almost. "Except for the cuteness part."

"Baloney!" Carrie said, and everybody knew, could tell, she'd had enough of people being serious, and *heavy*. "You're just saying that. Don't believe him, everybody. He's just trying to *score* on me, and, and . . . *borrow money* from the rest of you." She grabbed him by the shoulders, started shaking him. "I've known other kids like this; they never change."

In a moment, they were rolling down the slope, wrestling and laughing, both of them, each one trying to pin the other to the ground. Finally, Dennis ended up on top, holding both her wrists and straddling her body. He leaned forward, threatening—it seemed—to kiss her. He'd pushed his lips out, anyway.

"I take it back, I take it back!" cried Carrie, fake-repentant. "I didn't mean a word I said. He's good! He's changed! I promise everyone. I even think he's *cute*!"

Dennis smiled a Cheshire grin and let her go. She scrambled to her feet.

"Ee-*you*!" She made her most disgusted face. "He had his face right close to mine! He almost *kissed* me!" And she knelt beside the spring and washed her face with scooped-up double handfuls of the water.

In the confusion of those moments, Alec turned toward Elizabeth again, and reached, and took her hand in his. And shook his head and said, "I can't believe you said that."

She smiled (inscrutably, he might have thought), and squeezed his hand, and he was pretty sure she said, "Believe it, Alec."

And then *she* had to look away.

twenty-one

CISCO FINALLY AGREED to bring them all to Marius and Katya's. But he said they had to take precautions, try to play it safe.

"We'll wait till six or so," he said, "when all the neighbors ought to be inside, and loading up their plates. I'll go first, with Babylon, while the rest of you stay under cover, in the woods. If the coast is clear, and Marius and Katya say that it's okay, I'll sneak back out to the corral and wave you in."

The kids got all excited at the thought of going down into the valley, getting close to civilization, again. It wasn't exactly bright lights or a big city they were heading for, but it was *houses,* and some people other than the six of them.

Their first view of the village came in early afternoon, from up above. It surely wasn't big, consisting of no more than fifty buildings, total, on two crossing roads. All the houses faced the same direction, south. As everybody knew by then, this was so they'd catch the sun—in those glassed-in, porch-like areas where plants grew year-round, and on the solar panels on their roofs, the ones for heating water, and on the photovoltaic "shingles," which actually made each house's electricity. Almost every building had a garden plot beside it, some of them quite sizable, and over half of them had tanks or pools where fish were raised for eating. Unlike the houses in most rural villages on Earth, these didn't have a lot of cars and trucks outside them, obsolete or otherwise.

Everybody tried to pick out Marius and Katya's house. They figured it would be the biggest one in town, or at least the *grandest*. And Cisco'd *said* that it was on the edge of town, and had corrals around it. Because the town had just four edges (or eight, if you counted both sides of the two crossing roads), it shouldn't have been hard to guess their destination.

And it wasn't. Only one house on one edge had multiple corrals—or, in fact, *any* corrals—around it. And the corrals were impressive, as to size, some of them with barns beside them, some of them with donkeys and horses in them, and some containing cattle. What didn't meet their expectations in the slightest was the house itself. It wasn't big and white, or big and brick, or big and made of stone. Nor did it have a lot of rolling lawns and ornamental gardens and a swimming pool and tennis court, or even columns. It didn't have a gatehouse and a driveway leading up to it. In fact, the word it brought to Brenda's mind was . . . *cottage*.

Yes. In shape, it was a saltbox, meaning that it had two sloping roofs, the one in front a good deal less extensive than the one in back. It was made of rough-sawn planks of different widths and stained a mellow brown—although its window boxes, and the trim around the windows, and the doors were all pure white. There were trees and bushes on its lot—bushy evergreens in back and fruit trees out in front— and a fenced-in garden to one side. Little flower plots were scattered here and there. Although it wasn't big, the house looked solid, rooted, squatting there, underneath its widely overhanging eaves. The other word that came to Brenda's mind, the more she looked at it, was *cozy.*

"That's it?" said Carrie, pointing at the place, this cozy little cottage—this *cliché,* almost. There was a question in her voice, but also, certainly, amazement. Maybe even disappointment. "I give up."

"Yep," said Cisco. "Absolootle. What we'll do is stay back in the woods, right there"—he pointed to a spot quite near the donkey corral—"until it's time." He sounded boyish and excited, Brenda thought. Clearly, he was really looking forward to this visit.

"Should we eat before we get there?" asked the practical Elizabeth. "Make something now, and eat it cold down there? We still have macaroni left, and I could make some sauce with beans and oil and basil, and our two surviving onions."

"Naw," said Cisco. "I'm sure they'll want to feed us. Assuming that they let us in at all. Let's take our chances. We can always make that same meal later, if we have to. But, well, I guess I'm feeling lucky"—he held crossed fingers up—"now that we're so close to being there."

◆ ◆ ◆

And so, at six o'clock, or shortly after, he and Babylon (she without her saddlebags) strode purposefully across the fifty feet of open space between the woods and the corral. As Cisco opened up the gate for Babby, heads were turned their way and ears came up, but no one bawled or whinnied. Babylon herself seemed perfectly at home; she nodded once or twice, then headed for the water trough, and bellied up, and drank. Moments later, she was joined there, by some relatives and friends, presumably.

The watchers in the woods saw Cisco reach the house and bend to look in through a window. He seemed to knock on it, then wave, then go to the side door. It opened as he got to it, and Brenda was reminded of the night she'd watched him go to Josip and Marina's door and disappear inside. Then, he'd been a tall, dark stranger, attractive and mysterious— and unattainable. And now he was . . . a bosom friend, or something of the sort, at least. It was amazing how completely and how fast a person's life could change. Especially in Gypsyworld, it seemed.

About three minutes later, he came out again, and stood by the corral, and waved. There was no mistaking what he meant. Carrie thought of childhood games of hide-and-seek, and "Allee, allee, in free."

The kids went quickly and in single file, bent over. Duffy stayed by Carrie's side; Jackie chose to roost back in the woods. Dennis, who was first in line, headed for the door that Cisco'd disappeared inside, and as his fist went out to knock on it, it opened. There was Cisco, grinning broadly, with their host and hostess right behind him.

Later, Brenda said to Cisco that she saw, at once, why Marius and Katya got elected all those times.

"I guarantee you, I'd have voted for them," she maintained. "All you have to do is look at them to know that you can trust them. With your wallet, or your deepest, darkest secrets, I don't care. You know that right away. And then, besides, they look so *wise*."

Marius and Katya. Both of them were shorties—she about five one by Brenda's calculation, and he perhaps five inches taller. Her hair was thick and iron gray, and pulled back into a neat French twist; *his* round head was almost bald, with just a fringe of curly white, around the sides and back. They both had lovely skin, smooth except around their mouths and eyes—blue eyes, in Katya's case, and she was lighter than her husband. He was brown eyed and the color of a nicely grilled lamb chop.

Both of them wore glasses. His were big and owlish, black rimmed, perching on a stubby nose; she had pushed her wire rims up on her hair. They were dressed almost identically, in dark twill trousers and light-colored tailored shirts with sleeves rolled up above their elbows. Neither of them had on shoes; his socks were made of dark blue wool, and hers were flaming red. Both of them wore wristwatches, with faces and sweep second hands; she'd added earrings—bright enameled copper disks—and a necklace made of jade and garnet beads. Though certainly past seventy (by Brenda's estimate), they moved like younger people, one-time acrobats, perhaps—gracefully, with no apparent effort. Brenda thought that Katya weighed about a hundred pounds, and he no more than thirty over that.

"Welcome, welcome, welcome," both of them were saying, looking thrilled by what they saw, these five, strange, teenage kids.

"Leave your sneakers by the door," said Cisco, who was standing in a pair of rather ratty-looking argyles. Carrie tried to recollect if she had changed her socks, that morning.

The reasons for the no-shoes custom were apparent: the carpets, thick and bright and colorful, in various designs. Brenda'd never seen a group of rugs like that; she thought that they'd be worth a fortune, back on Earth.

They covered much of the first floor—basically, a big square open area, minus one north corner where the bathroom was. The kitchen setup was along one side, stove, refrigerator, sink and counters; most of the rest was living-dining space. There was a big refectory table, with eight captain's chairs; for reading and relaxing there were cushioned chairs and one huge, sink-in sofa. Glazed vases holding fresh-cut flowers were on every other table. A curtained corner seemed to be a sleeping alcove; in another corner, there were stairs.

"I expect you're hungry," Katya said. "Hiking builds *my* appetite, I know. So, we'll be sitting down to eat in . . . how long, Mari? Fifteen minutes? Twenty?"

"More like twenty," he replied. He rubbed his hands together. When they'd come in, he'd gone from kid to kid, shaking each one's hand, and looking straight into each person's eyes, and saying, for example, "You, I think, are Carrie. Yes? I'm very glad to meet you, Carrie." (When Brenda took his hand, she had a lovely feeling: Cisco'd *told* him something; this man *knows*.) Now, he quickly turned and went into the kitchen area and soon was running water into two big pots, and saying "Twenty at the *least,* I'd say."

"Both of us enjoy to cook," said Katya, "and tonight the honor fell to him."

"Bad luck for our good guests," he called, and chuckled.

"Meanwhile," Katya said. She moved into the sitting area. "We have the bathroom over there. You'll be sleeping on the second floor; feel free to look around. There's juice from local apples in the fridge, for now or later." She looked around and smiled. "And Cisco, I should hope, remembers where the dishes and the napkins are."

People moved this way and that. Elizabeth went over to the kitchen, and she soon was washing lettuce in the sink. Brenda followed Cisco to the cabinets and drawers where tableware was kept; the bowls and plates and forks and knives were heavy and unusual, she thought, made both for looks and durability. The napkins were wine-colored cloth. Alec walked around the room, looking at the prints and paintings on the barnboard walls. At one point, he announced that *he* would do the dishes, after; "I got *dibs* on them," he said. Dennis found the apple juice and glasses. He poured one full and carried it to Katya, leaving Carrie standing by the fridge, and gaping.

In slightly less than *thirty* minutes, they were at the table, ravenous, for sure. Dinner was the most gigantic salad any of the kids had ever seen, so big it had to go in two huge wooden bowls.

"Kitchen sink salad, is the name of what it is," said Marius. "Besides three kinds of lettuce, there are hard-cooked eggs, and cheese, cold beans and rice, and fresh-steamed vegetables. No cukes because I have distastes for them, and no toe-*mahts* because I have forgot them! House dressing by Elizabeth, you luckies!"

There were also two hot loaves of bread, and a crock of butter. Everybody had a glass of apple juice, and Katya raised hers to the table, when she saw that everyone was served.

"*Salut,*" she said. "Once again: we're *very* glad you come."

Everybody did as she did, holding up their glasses, first to her and then to Marius and saying, "Thanks for having us," "We're glad we're here," and so on. When Brenda heard that word, *salut,* and recognized the French (of course), she realized she'd forgotten to employ *her* French for . . . days and days. She began to wonder why that was, and found she didn't care.

♦ ♦ ♦

Listening to Katya, and to Marius, the way they talked to people during dinner, Brenda felt relaxed—and envious, a little. She hoped that *she* could be like Katya, someday: confident, informed, but in a gentle, not a show-off, kind of way. It seemed that she and Marius (like Josip and Marina, come to think of it) had figured out what mattered and what didn't—what stuff they couldn't do a thing about, and what they might affect. She didn't think that they were *worried* over anything.

It was clear, right from the start, that Cisco'd told their hosts the basics of their story, the whos and whats and whens and hows and whys. It was also very clear their hosts were sympathetic, and they wanted to be helpful. Any way they could be.

"Are you much exhausted after all these days on trail?" asked Katya, at one point. She looked down the table at her husband. "Should we, maybe, *drive* them to the border? We could take a day for that?"

As Marius began to smile and shake his head, Dennis, sitting at her right, got curious. "You have a van?" he asked. "Like Josip and Marina?"

"Oh," said Marius, "we haven't any auto*mobile,* no. And that thing of Josip and Marina wasn't *theirs*—belongs to Gypsyworld, all people. Katya meant the horse cart, I imagine."

There was a little silence after that.

"Oh, a *horse cart,*" Alec said. He did his nervous laugh. "Do you know I've never even *seen* one?" And, when no one answered that, he kept on babbling.

"That's such a major difference, here," he said. "Having people not drive cars a lot. At home, for kids our age, that's like a major milestone. Learning how to drive, getting your own car—that kind of thing."

"Don't tell me—*you* know how to drive a car?" said Katya. "All of you have driven cars? With engines that burn fossil fuels?" She sounded both incredulous and horrified.

Everybody nodded, everybody but Elizabeth. "We learn in school," said Alec.

"I'm not meant to," Dennis said, "but I can. My uncle showed me."

"Good Lord," said Katya. "That is so . . . unfortunate. I didn't know the situation was so bad, still, where you live; we get so out of touch. Ourselves, we'd never drive a vehicle like that. I mean, a *Ford,* is it? Or Cadillac? Our kids would have a fit, and rightly so."

"What?" said Carrie, and she laughed. "Kids tell their *parents* what to do, in Gypsyworld?"

"No no no no no no," said Marius, and he laughed, too. "Gypsy parents not completely screw-loose, Carrie. What Katya means is something else. Relationship between the generations. You have to understand: No one here cares much about accumulation. We don't go for lots of this and that—*consumer* goods, I think they say on Earth—just enough to satisfy our needs. We don't throw much away, and we enjoy the durable, and beautiful, and well-made (often *hand*made) things we have." He lifted up the plate that he was eating from. "These dishes go three generations back, some carpets many more than that. We don't go shopping very much, and no one has a want for lots of money."

"But we do have something very valuable to leave our kids," said Katya. "Namely, Gypsyworld—this wondrous place we live in. Our duty, and our happiness as well, is that we pass it on to them as good or better than we got it from *our* parents."

"How selfish and how evil it would be," said Marius, "for

us to use it up, or hurt it, so that their heritage was less than ours. You understand?"

Brenda nodded. She was *sure* she did. This wasn't preaching she was hearing, someone being holier-than-thou, or telling her about some goal that (in a word) was unattainable. These were simple, reasonable facts. They didn't make it sound like any great big deal—just something necessary, logical, and *so*.

"I was wondering," said Alec. "Do you have an army here in Gypsyworld? On Earth, as I suppose you know, most countries spend a fortune on defense—armies, weapons, all that sort of stuff. If people here don't have a lot of money, that would mean they can't be taxed a lot, and *that* would mean there wouldn't be a way to pay for all those military things. But maybe you don't think you *need* an army. I was wondering."

"We hope we don't," said Katya. "No, we have no army, just a modest national police. Citizens—civilians—help them out, like now." She smiled. "To look for you. Most of us are not concerned about our borders with your countries, usually. They're very hard to . . . locate, from the other side. And besides, this country isn't rich in anything, except for quality of life."

"Speaking of exactly that," said Cisco, "I am *pooped*." He rose and stretched. "Would it be all right for us to do the dishes now—"

"*My* job!" cried Alec. "I got dibs—remember?"

"—so that the ones who want to head for bed can shortly do so?" Cisco finished. "I'm thinking that we ought to take off at the crack of dawn tomorrow, before the town starts stirring. Oh, and thanks for offering, but honestly, we'd rather walk."

"Whatsoever you prefer," said Marius, nodding his agreement. "And anyone who wants, tonight—warm shower, eh? With all the sun we had today, there should be plenty of hot water. Or, *almost* plenty, anyway."

There was another flurry of activity. Dishes were carefully stacked and taken to the sink. Katya pulled a spice cake from a cabinet, and made some herbal tea. People moved in various directions—toward the bathroom, toward the sink, upstairs and down again, back to the table with a piece of cake. Dish towels were exchanged; bath towels appeared; Marius and Katya were required to sit down and let their guests take care of them.

Brenda saw that they had *really* "made themselves at home," Cisco and the five of them, without the slightest awkwardness. And that that was due to Marius and Katya, and the way the two of them had made them—*let* them— feel. Not like kids but, simply, fellow human beings. Fellow *gypsies,* even.

◆ ◆ ◆

By quarter after nine that night, the six of them were all upstairs, on feather mattresses laid side by side on one room's floor. The room was perfect for their purposes, in terms of spaciousness. There were also hooks for clothes, a nice big mirror, chairs, a dresser and two stacks of mattresses and quilts.

Just before he fell asleep, Alec touched Elizabeth, who was beside him, on the shoulder. Her necklace made a little clicking sound as she rolled over.

"What?" she said. Her little whisper barely made a sound.

"The point?" He breathed the word in her direction,

lying on his side; this was just for her to hear. "That *point* Marina talked about? I think I may . . . well, it's a *feeling*, don't you think? About . . . well, *everyone* and . . . I guess you'd call it *nature,* and . . ." He felt her fingers on his face. They found his lips and stayed there; he tried to, dared to— sort of—kiss them.

After that, she might have whispered something. Then, before she took her hand away. Or maybe she just sighed. He wasn't sure, and wasn't going to ask her to repeat it. If those *had* been whispers that he heard, she *might* have said both "Yes," and then "I love you."

◆ ◆ ◆

The next thing Brenda knew, Cisco's hand was on her shoulder, shaking her awake. It was almost totally pitch dark. He had his flashlight on, but kept his fingers over it in such a way that hardly any light came out. From the other side of him, she heard some mutters, and (perhaps) the sound of people sitting up.

"What time is it?" she asked.

Instead of answering, he leaned way over her. "Alec?" he said then. "Elizabeth? You both awake?"

"Yes," she heard, from both of them.

"It's twenty after one," said Cisco, then. "And here's the deal. There've been . . . developments. I got this all from Marius just now, downstairs."

Brenda was amazed. That feather mattress must have really done a job on her. He'd gotten up, from right beside her, gone downstairs and come back up, and she had never stirred.

"Sometime after we retired," Cisco said, "Marius and Katya's son dropped in. Emil—he's a nice guy, pest control biologist, lives right here in town. He didn't come for any special reason, just to visit, have a cup of tea; I guess he's apt to do that once or twice a week. Well, anyway, at some point he just mentioned—totally offhandedly, they said—that he had heard a rumor, earlier. Concerning us—or you, I *should* say. The rumor was: you might be hiding in the village, here. And, furthermore, that different groups of searchers had been moving into place, to block all exits from the valley. And tomorrow they were going to do a house-to-house, to look for you. That'd be *today,* of course."

"Cripes," said Dennis, from the darkness. "What're we gonna do? Is there someplace to hide, that Marius and Katya know? Or do we make a run for it? Or what?" He sounded wide awake, and angry, ready for some action, Brenda thought.

"Marius has been outside already," Cisco said. "He did some scouting here and there; he thinks the rumor's right. A bunch of people have the routes we could have taken blocked."

"Damn," said Alec. "It's not that I'm so anxious to get home." He moved one hand a little in the dark, toward Elizabeth; she found it. "But if they capture us, I just don't see how we'll *convince* them that—"

Cisco interrupted him. "Wait," he said. "I think that there's a chance we can escape. Old Marius, he knows a million tricks; he has an . . . interesting plan. I'll tell you while you're getting dressed. He's out there now, by the corrals."

twenty-two

WHEN THEY GOT OUTSIDE, they stopped beside the cattle pen to say good-bye to Marius. He was busy, still, inside it. In the weak light coming from the stars, the kids could barely see his shape, in there.

"This is the *most* in-*ge*-ni-ous idea I've ever—" Alec started. But the old man interrupted him.

"How does the saying go?" he asked. "The best-made plan of mouse and man . . . ? Don't credit me until it's worked, my Alec. We shall see—or *you* will—soon enough."

"We wait until they're off the road, before we turn the thingees on," said Cisco. "Right? And you're completely sure they *will* get off."

"Yes," said Marius. "Of course. These are good old cows; they have the habits of a lifetime. That's the way they go to pasture, and they always will, every chance they get. Don't worry. It's *after,* comes the hard part. Waiting for our friends up there to take off after them. It may be ten or fifteen, even twenty minutes. It all depends how good their lookout is. And how long it takes to rouse the ones who sleep. You sure you don't want me to come—and wait with you?"

"No, really—there's no reason," Cisco said. "Better you should be at home. You never know; you might be telephoned, or something. You can say you were asleep, and that they must have come and stole your cows, the little devils." And he laughed.

"So thanks a million times for this, the food, the hospitality, the *everything*," continued Cisco. "You and Katya are the best. If it's okay, we'll also grab some feed for Babylon, as we depart. That'll keep her quiet while they're going by us."

"Assuming that they do," said Marius. He made a little grunt. "Okay, all finished. Assuming that they bite." He came out of the cattle pen. They heard the gate squeak, and then there he was.

"The best of luck, my boy," he said. And he and Cisco wrapped their arms around each other.

"And to all of you sweet people," he continued, moving toward the rest of them.

Brenda was glad she was the nearest to him, after Cisco. Hugging this amazing, sweet old man was no more difficult or awkward than . . . well, hugging Cisco would be. And Carrie and Elizabeth, in the dimness after her, were also sentimental, feeling females.

What she couldn't have predicted—and what almost knocked her over, never mind the feather—was the way that Dennis and then Alec grabbed ahold of Marius, as if this thing of hugging other males was something they'd been doing all their lives. It wasn't that they did it *smoothly* (Alec, though perhaps a prince, would always be part frog), but even in that dimness she could see they did it absolutely heartily, and without the least embarrassment or hesitation.

"Good-bye, good-bye, good-bye," said everyone, as Marius reopened the pen's gate and let the five cows out.

The big brown animals did not take time to look around or get their bearings. Moving slowly and sedately, they simply started strolling down the road, as they had done so many times before. The little flashlights Marius had taped to each of their left horns seemed to be of no concern to them at all—although of course they weren't on, not yet. As usual, the animals walked in a line, a little ways apart, as Marius had said they would.

Cisco and Elizabeth, meanwhile, collected Babylon and Jackie, so it wasn't long before the six and their three animals (Jackie riding on a shoulder) were moving down the road in starlight, following the cows.

◆　◆　◆

About half a mile from where they started, the road began to turn a little left, and very shortly after, it was going uphill, too. Cisco picked up his pace, at that point. Marius had said that it was just a little ways uphill where they would leave the road to angle upward on a cow path, the one that took them to high pasture. He wanted to be ready when that happened.

He wasn't, quite, but he was close enough. He could see the lead cow, not too far in front of him, when suddenly she *did* veer right, and off the road, and onto a dirt track. Another dozen steps and he was up beside her head, and flicking on the little flashlight on her horn. Marius had taped it so it angled down, and hit the path that she was walking on. As each succeeding cow came up to him, he did the same for her, and all five lights worked perfectly.

Then Cisco held his breath; he thought this was a crucial moment. For the cows, this was a first, a very new experience—a lighted path. No one could know for sure that they would tolerate this change in their routine. It was possible they wouldn't—that they'd try to scrape the flashlights off, against a tree, or, worse yet, that they'd stop and shine their lights on one another, maybe talk things over for a while.

Those possibilities did not take place, however. All of them reacted . . . not at all; or, "bovinely," perhaps. They ignored both him and what he'd caused to happen, totally. Keeping to the same determined pace, the five continued up the hill, entirely unaware (of course) that they'd become a feature of the evening landscape—not they themselves, but those five bobbing little lights, ascending at an angle through the hillside darkness.

As Marius had said, however, there was still a very hard part, coming up. While the cows continued on their way, Cisco and the kids and their three animals went off the road as well, but on the other side of it. There was a grove of scrubby trees that perched on a small knoll, from which they could observe the road, while also being hidden from it. All (*some* all!) they had to do was wait and hope the searchers' lookout, up above, would see the moving lights and draw the obvious conclusion: that those five dangerous kids were trying to escape the valley. That, thinking everybody else would be asleep, they'd started on a bold cross-country journey in the dark. Probably the little dopes had no idea they were trapped there in that valley.

Five minutes passed, then ten. The animals were lying down, except for Jackie, and the people all were sitting near them and to one another, listening, afraid to make a sound. Also afraid they wouldn't *hear* a sound.

Two minutes more went by, then suddenly the searchers, all on bicycles, came whooshing down the road with flashlights of their own in hand, so fast they missed the path the cows had taken. But Cisco didn't doubt they'd find it coming back.

"Let's go," he said, and, leading Babby, he was up and heading for the road. "Let's *hustle*. Maybe also say a prayer they didn't leave some people at the top, all right? Once we're out of here and in the woods again, I guarantee they'll never, *ever* find us."

And he turned and grinned a grin that Brenda'd never seen before, and liked at once: a slightly wicked and triumphant one.

She trotted to catch up to him, and when she did, she threw an arm around his neck and kissed him on the cheek. With all the great things that had happened lately, she felt they had a lot to celebrate.

twenty-three

THREE MORNINGS LATER, they were there, as far as Cisco planned to take them. "There" was a surprise; it didn't look at all the way that Brenda had expected it would.

For one thing, it was not a place with gates that lifted up, and guards, a "border" like the ones you see in movies or on television. It, the border, was a distance farther on, eight miles about, said Cisco. There was a road that led from "there" to it, a gray cement road in superb condition all the way (he told them); it was as good a road as they had seen, in Gypsyworld. From where they were, they could see the road go roller-coastering away, across an arid landscape. There were some bushes and some scrubby pines on either side of it, and good-sized boulders, too—a little shade, in other words, and water not that far below the surface, probably. And there were gullies, cut into the land, where lots of water rushed on through at some time of the year, not this one. It was hotter there than anyplace they'd been in Gypsyworld.

"A lot of immigrants still use this route, as well as truckers with supplies," said Cisco. "We still import a fair amount of stuff from Earth, though less and less, each year.

It's a good way to come *in* the country, if you know how to come in at all. But people seldom leave this way. No one would ever think that you—five foreigners—could even *find* this route for getting out of here. There aren't any signs, of course, and right until you're there, it doesn't look as if you're going anywhere—except across a semidesert."

They were doing their looking from the shelter of the forest, still. They'd been hiking through the forest, very much as usual, and it was getting close to noon, around the time they often stopped for lunch. No one had suspected they were getting close to anywhere, when—bingo! Just ahead, it seemed there was a clearing, or the far edge of the forest—in any case, an open area. Cisco'd said it simply: "Well, we're here." And so they were.

Besides the "semidesert" and the road that ran off into it, there were other things for them to look at, most surprising things.

In the first place, there was quite a good-sized diner, the first such structure that they'd seen in Gypsyworld, with a big sign saying EAT, out front. Beside it was a little building that resembled Marius and Katya's house, but painted white and even smaller. The sign outside *it* said REST AND INFORMATION AREA.

In back of that, there was (amazingly) a kind of used-car lot. Inside its chain-link fence—the gate of which was propped wide open—there was a large array of vehicles of different types and sizes. Some of them were long and shiny and appeared to be the kinds of cars you'd see a lot of in some neighborhoods on Earth. Like, in Beverly Hills, California, or outside country clubs in Tulsa, or Las Vegas, or East Hampton. These were the cars (as Cisco knew) that certain immigrants to Gypsyworld had driven into it, and then had realized where they were, and—yes—remembered why they'd come. And promptly traded in before a lot of gypsies saw them. Another row of vehicles were more like those that Brenda'd seen when she walked into town that day, and first met Cisco by the bus stop. They were smaller, much more fuel-efficient cars, some of them electric—also, panel trucks. There was also quite a row of two- and three-wheeled vehicles, some of which had little trailers hooked on them: motorcycles, ATVs, mopeds, and a huge variety of bicycles. The sign outside the lot said VICTOR'S VEHICLES— BUY/SELL/TRADE/RENT—STATUS SYMBOLS CHEERFULLY ACCEPTED.

What there didn't seem to be in Victor's was a single customer, or salesperson. But then, there wasn't any evidence that anyone was in the diner, either. Or in the Rest and Information Area.

Alec was the one who checked his watch.

"Aha," he said. "It's Sunday!"

"Yep," said Cisco, "and there isn't anybody here. There isn't anybody here on Tuesday or on Thursday, either. There's only four days of the week that people go to Earth, or come from there. That's something we agreed upon two years ago, I think it was. To cut down on the goings and the comings. To sort of wean ourselves away from Earth."

"Interesting," Alec said. He laughed, but not good humoredly. "I'd say that's pretty smart of you—considering how screwed up things have gotten, there." He paused and added, loyally, "Not everything, of course, but lots of stuff."

"So, what's the deal?" asked Dennis. He shifted weight from one foot to the other, and gave his pack a hitch. "We gonna just head out? Go down that road until we get to . . . what?"

"You'll see," said Cisco. "It isn't difficult, or complicated, just a little . . . strange, unusual. Like Alice going down that rabbit hole. But I thought we'd have some lunch and stuff right here, before you left."

Brenda thought: Well, I should hope so. A lot of things still needed to be talked about, explained, perhaps decided on. She and Cisco'd hugged and whispered back and forth the last two nights, excited by the fact that they were going to spend the next six months together. But no one else knew that; they all assumed that she'd be going back to Earth with them. What if someone else—Elizabeth, for instance—asked if she could also stay? How would Cisco answer that one? *She* didn't even know how she would want him to.

People started getting food out; there was bread and cheese from Katya's, still, and Dennis went for water. No one's mood seemed light or lively. Now that they were getting close to home, there was a tension and excitement in the air, but sadness, too.

Elizabeth had taken out a folded piece of paper from her pack. On its outside, she had written *Josip and Marina*.

"Could you deliver this to them?" She held the paper out to Cisco. "It's a letter." She turned to all the others. "It tells them that I wish I could have stayed. Remember when they said that they'd adopted us? Well, me, I wish I could have *stayed* adopted, kept on living here, with them." She stopped talking suddenly. Brenda'd never seen her look so miserable, not since that first day, there in the Winnebago van.

"I would've stayed here, too," said Alec, softly, "if I could've."

Elizabeth looked over at him. "You really would have?" It

sounded like she really *had to* know. Her eyes were large and shiny.

"Yes, I absolutely would have." Alec smiled his geeky smile at her. He took a breath. "Partly just to be with you. I'm not going to try to deny it." He checked expressions on the other faces in the group. Everyone (except Elizabeth) was nibbling at bread and cheese and listening to him, but no one looked to be about to laugh, or make a wise remark. "But also, just because of how it is here, in this country. Of course I still don't know a lot about it. Like I said before, maybe people here would hate me, I don't know. But if I could, I'd take that chance."

"Yeah," said Dennis, nodding. "Those kids that I was shooting baskets with—they weren't what I'd call the *coolest* bunch I've ever met. I know what you're saying, though. The grown-ups here have all been neat and, face it, Cisco, here, is *perfect*—right?" He leaned across and, grinning, slapped him on the shoulder. His voice was overloud, again. "But that still don't mean we'd get along—like, if we moved here, ever. *Possibly* we would, but we don't know."

"Well, the fact is," Carrie said, "we *can't* live here, except in jail. I agree with everyone who thinks it might be better in a place like this, *healthier* for sure, but honey"—she was looking at Elizabeth—"we don't have a choice. If we stayed here, when they caught up with us—who *knows* what they might do?"

"I *know* that," said Elizabeth. "I just had to tell them—Josip and Marina—what I *felt*."

"Um, maybe somehow," Brenda said to Cisco, "once the other gypsies realize we escaped, and haven't led a lot of people in across the border, maybe they'll all change their minds. And have a different attitude about . . . well, kids from Earth. Don't you think that's possible?"

She'd said "*we* escaped" intentionally. She thought it might make Cisco contradict her, say she wasn't going, tell the other ones about the six months deal. But even if he didn't, she'd had a reason for the question, too. She hoped that in a while the others *could* come back. She hoped that all of them could keep on being friends.

"Sure," he said. "I really do. In fact, I hope to make it happen. Once all of you are safely out of here"—Brenda thought he *could* have winked, as he said that—"I'm going to *go* to the Assembly and tell them . . . that we spent some time together, in the woods—of course I didn't know that you were *wanted*—and that I got to know you really well." Now he was smiling broadly, first at her and then at all the rest of them. "I hope that they'll *invite* you back, no kidding."

"But, wait," said Dennis. "Let's suppose they did. How would we find out? Can I call you on the phone somewhere, or something?"

Cisco laughed. "Unfortunately not," he said. "We haven't got that kind of link with Earth." He thought a second, held a finger up. "But, hey! I can always come on a permitted travel day, and *tell* you all the news. Yeah, that's a great idea! Suppose I said I'd be . . . oh, how about outside your public library, downtown, a week from Monday? How would that be? I might even bring a friend." (I guess he's finally leading up to telling them, thought Brenda.)

"That'd be *fantastic,*" Dennis said. He looked at all the others. "Wouldn't it? See ol' buddy Cisco—what?—eight days from now, and hear if we've been—whachacallit?—*pardoned,* would it be? Maybe we could come on back, right then."

Everybody looked enthusiastic, everyone but Alec. He was picking at his piece of bread, making little bread balls out of it, and scowling at the ground. His glasses, unattended, had slid down his nose.

"Alec? Alec?" Dennis said. "What gives?"

The tall boy's curly head came up; he pushed the glasses back where they belonged.

"What?" he said. "Oh, sorry." And he flashed his grin, apologetically. "I just remembered something. Something pretty bad—about today. *Some* of us, and we don't know which ones, were *sold* to Josip and Marina. I suppose they would have told the ones who were, eventually, and helped them make . . . *arrangements* to live somewhere else. But now, the way things are, two or three of us are going to walk in our front doors today and not be . . . well, exactly welcome."

No one spoke up right away. A few mouths opened slightly, and at least one lip was chewed. Every kid, including Brenda, thought about how it would be to walk in your front door and see amazement on your parents' faces. Followed, probably, by fear. *And* loathing. *Fury.*

That would not be just an awful situation; it would be a dangerous one, as well.

"Um, maybe all of us, before we actually go in our house, should sort of ask around, ask other kids," said Carrie. "Wouldn't . . . well, our *friends* and other people— *neighbors*—know how they reacted, how our parents did, I mean, to having us, well, *disappear?* Like, for instance, if I heard my mother bought new clothes and went out dancing all the time, maybe I'd just go and stay at Alec's place."

That got Brenda thinking, really thinking. Although she'd said to Carrie that she thought her parents might have sold her to the King and Queen, she'd never been *convinced* of that. She'd had a ton of hassles with her parents, sure, but in her heart of hearts she thought, believed, that she was one of those who had been stolen. Obnoxious as it was, her parents' nagging was "for her own good"; she was sure that was the way *they* looked at it, at least. She was *pretty* sure they'd never given up on her, and *that* meant that they'd never sell her, didn't it? Probably, her disappearance . . . broke their hearts. Really *devastated* them.

But if she'd been going home that night, the way the others were . . . well, then she might have taken some precautions. Possibly along the lines that Carrie had suggested. None of them was such a perfect piece of work that he or she could say, *for sure,* "It isn't me."

"The only trouble is," said Alec, "anyone who actually *did* sell their kid . . . If they were in the least bit smart, they would have made a real big show of calling up the cops, and everything—reporting that their kid had run away, or something, don't you think? And they'd surely put another big act on, just for the neighbors. Later on, they'd spend the money, maybe on a trip 'to try to take their minds off everything that happened.' " He said the last part in a different tone of voice, and really sounded bitter.

Dennis was the one who'd had his lip between his teeth.

"Cripes, this *is* a mess," he said. "I'm scared. Somebody could get hurt, real bad." He looked at Carrie. "You know what *I* vote? I vote, when we get back to Earth, that *none* of us goes home. I vote we stick together, keep on camping out like we've been doing." He looked at Cisco. "If we could keep our sleeping bags and stuff, we *could* do that, I bet— find someplace out of town. And then on Monday, if you came real early, you could tell us if we even *had* a choice— like, if we *could* come back, or what."

Brenda looked around at all the other kids and they were

nodding. What Dennis said made sense. The situation *was* a mess. No one could be positive that it was safe to go back home, no matter what the neighbors said. She supposed the King and Queen had been so sure that this experiment would work that they hadn't even *thought* about this possibility. They must have just assumed that all of them—the ones they'd stolen *and* the ones they'd bought—would have the choice to stay right there in Gypsyworld, happily, forever after. They would have planned to break the news, themselves, to whoever it was they'd bought. Brenda was sure they'd have done that in a really thoughtful, gentle way.

And then she looked at Cisco. He was nodding, too, but he looked ashen, kind of horrified. Although she couldn't know for sure, she bet that he'd been struck by more or less the same thoughts she'd just had. Except in his case it was . . . well, his *parents* (parents who he clearly loved, a lot) who had (unintentionally, of course) put some of them in mortal danger (possibly). For the second time, he was having to deal with an unpleasant truth: that though his parents' goal (of saving Earth) was wonderful and noble, they had used some methods, trying to reach that goal, that weren't only thoughtless, but were downright *wrong*.

And then she realized something else. If the other four were going to stick together, back on Earth, *she* should go and stick together with them. It would be wrong of *her* to stay and just let Cisco hide her and take care of her, enjoy herself, while they, the other four, were camping out and sweating out the word from Gypsyworld.

Like it or not—and she had come to *love* it, just about—they'd become a unit, there: "those five kids from Earth." She'd never had a special group of friends like that, before.

She told herself that Cisco'd understand. He had a job to

do she couldn't help him with. The others needed her a whole lot more than he did. In eight days' time, she'd head on back to Gypsyworld with him, no matter how it all turned out. Well, wouldn't she? She felt a little sick, and more in love with him than ever.

Next, she took a big deep breath and shook her head. To hell with that idea. She'd stay with him, as planned; her going back to Earth would be ridiculous. A person had to take care of herself, look out for number one. No one else is going to do that *for* a person; that's the kind of world it is.

But then she looked at Alec, Carrie, Dennis and Elizabeth. And thought: Is that the kind of world I want to be a part of?

"I know exactly where we'll camp," she said, before her mind could think again. "There's this place up on the cliffs, above the beach I go to all the time. It's really wild, but not that far from town. And it'll be a cinch for him to find." She'd thought that she could feel his eyes on her, as soon as she'd said "we'll."

She turned and put a hand down on his knee.

"It'll only be eight days. We'll be okay," she said. "All right?"

He didn't answer right away. He seemed exhausted. But then he said, "Uh-huh, you're right. That *is* the best idea. Why, by a week from Monday, the Assembly will probably be *begging* you to please come back. I'll have personally guaranteed your, your . . ."—he stammered, looking for a word—"your *lovability,* to them." And he began to nod.

"Sure, you guys keep your packs and stuff," he said. "I may even have some dollars, from the last time that I went to Earth." He got up, a little like a zombie; he was looking at his watch. He went to rummage in his saddlebags.

His looking at his watch just underlined a painful truth; everybody knew that it was time to go. They'd said the things that needed to be said, and there wasn't any point in hanging out, and dragging out good-byes. No one was in a real good mood.

"So, all we have to do is walk eight miles across a desert," Carrie started. "With our packs and—"

"Walk?" said Dennis, interrupting. "Hey, to hell with that. Walk, with wheels available at Victor's, there?" He pointed. "We can ditch whatever we decide to borrow by the border. That'd be okay, right, Cisco? And maybe you could pay the rental for us, later, right?"

Cisco shrugged and kept on searching in the saddlebag. Brenda hoped he was okay. She sort of wished that she could tell him how upset *she* was, by this change of plans. But then she asked herself what purpose that would serve. *She* knew *he* knew she was right in going back. And that she wanted, more than anything, to be with him. She'd made that clear enough, the last two days. She sure *hoped* she had.

"Well." He finally turned back from the saddlebags. He had a wad of money, not a big one, in his hand. And tears were streaming down his face.

◆　◆　◆

In the main room of the Rest and Information Area, in that not-so-big white cottage with the diner on one side of it and Victor's Vehicles in back, the atmosphere was . . . *loaded,* Josip thought. Loaded, first of all, with all the . . . *emanations* from eleven adult bodies sitting in close quarters on the floor of one small room that only had two windows open, just a crack. And loaded, in the second place, with expectations that, in some four hours' waiting time, had partly curdled into boredom, blame and (yes!) exasperation.

In addition to Marina and himself, and Anwar, Carlo and Finita, there were the six hard-liners from the Gypsy-world Assembly, led by Ugo and Sofia. Josip and Marina had collected them at dawn, nearly certain this would be the day (the place, as well) the kids would try to cross the border. They'd had a call from Katya that informed them where the six had been two days before. And all along they'd known that Cisco'd take them to the border on a Sunday, or a Tuesday, or a Thursday; he was, after all, their son, and smart enough to choose a day when no one else would be around.

The King and Queen and all their guests had gotten to the cottage a little after eight a.m. The mood inside the Winnebago, driving up, had been both curious and dubious—and hopeful, Josip thought. These were gypsies, face it. They recognized a good plan and a fair test when they heard one, and the planners *were* their King and Queen. Even Ugo and Sofia were prepared to keep their minds a little open, anyway, and see what happened. But now, four hours later, they were doubtful and uncomfortable; they wanted out of there. In the last half hour, Ugo had begun to *speak,* instead of whisper. Anytime now, Josip thought, Sofia might chime in and say, "*I* don't think they're coming, and I've still got dinner to prepare. Let's get out of here."

He looked over at Marina, hoping she was working out a counterploy. What if they promised they would treat her to a nice pan pizza, with "the works," for every member of her family?

But his wife was staring out a window, toward the woods, and pointing. The pointer finger of her other hand was pressed against her lips.

"Shhh," she went, and whispered, "here they come."

The eleven all got on their knees and, biting back on

grunts, shuffled into prearranged positions by the windows that looked out the back. By staying on the floor, like that, they didn't think they could be seen by anyone outside. And with two windows cracked, there even was a chance they'd overhear some conversation.

Josip and Marina's gamble had begun.

◆　◆　◆

The kids came quickly, straight across the diner's parking lot; Victor's seemed to be their destination, sure enough. Josip and Marina thought they saw a difference in them right away. They didn't slouch or straggle. All of them had packs slung over their right shoulders, and they looked alert and fit. Even Alec, moving, didn't any longer have that total rag-doll look. But when the kids got close, the watchers saw that some of them were clutching hand-kerchiefs, and all of them, apparently, had recently been crying.

The kids went into Victor's through the open gate, and began to look around. There was the sound of noses being blown, and heads were shaken.

Nearest to the gate there was that row of recent imports, cars some gypsy immigrants had used to come from Earth. Some of them were junk, but some were beauties. For example: a Lincoln Town Car, 1991 (V8, blk, auto, leather, air); a '90 Volvo 760 TGA (White/Beige, Lthr, Auto, A/C, Sunroof); an '87 ½ Rolls Royce Corniche Convertible (Laguna Blue w. Magnolia Interior); a '92 Mercedes 560SEC Coupe (Pearl Grey/Grey Leather, 5.6 liter 8 cyl), a '90 Cadillac Allante (hardtop, red w/charcoal, AM/FM Ster Cass), even a recent Bentley Turbo R.

"Jeez mareez," they all heard Dennis say, "some gypsies

must be *millionaires*—at least back where they came from. Look." He pointed at the license plates. "New York, New Jersey, Texas, California . . . What's that? France? And over there: Zaire and Bangladesh."

Carrie was peering in the Bentley's window.

"Just once," she said, real slowly, "just once I'd like to drive this through the parking lot, down at my old school." She sounded wistful, tired too, fed up. She turned away and slapped the Cadillac's front fender.

"Hey, Alec," she called over to him. "Think that you'd have any trouble getting dates if you had one of these?" Her laughter sounded fake, like someone trying for a different mood, but not succeeding with the effort.

He came over, stuck his head inside the Caddy's window.

"Well," he said, "they left the keys inside, so maybe I'll find out . . ." He looked over his left shoulder to be sure Elizabeth was listening. But when he saw she was, he added, "But of course I'm only kidding."

"All of them have keys in them," said Carrie, walking down the line of cars. "Just think. *All* of us could take one home—except for you, Elizabeth, poor kid." She turned and walked back to the Bentley, with her arms apart.

"Come to momma, baby." And she went to its front door and stroked the handle.

"You going to take it?" Dennis asked. "There's no one here to stop you, and I s'pose if it got *in* here, it could make it out, all right. You gonna take that one? If you do, I'll take the Lincoln, there."

Everybody, then, was standing still; all of them were near a different car, except for small Elizabeth, who'd gone to Alec's side. Now they were holding hands. Only Dennis looked at Carrie.

She didn't keep them in suspense.

"Right. Sure," she said. "You jerk. I swear, you're *hope-less*. Haven't you learned *anything*?"

She turned and walked away from him and from the car, across the lot. Now she was really laughing, but not bitterly or meanly. (Brenda smiled to hear what she was hearing, once again: Carrie's "gotcha" laugh.) There wasn't any doubt about which vehicles of Victor's she was heading for.

Dennis's voice came after her.

"*You're* the jerk," he said. "The *idiot*. I was *kidding*, moron. Can't you recognize a joke? I swear, it's lucky you're nice looking, 'cause if you ever had to make it on your brains . . ."

By that time, all of them were going in the same direction, toward the long, long rack with all the different bicycles in it.

◆ ◆ ◆

Inside the Rest and Information Area, they'd heard all that, and the smiles on Josip's and Marina's faces went from ear to ear. And everybody else was nodding.

◆ ◆ ◆

Cisco had waited in the shelter of the woods, leaning sideways up against a tree. He knew he couldn't leave till they were out of sight. Duff was sitting at his feet, looking back and forth between the distant kids and him; from time to time, he made a tiny little whimper sound.

It didn't take long for all the kids to choose their bikes, and they were wheeling them toward Victor's gate when Josip and Marina and the other nine appeared, from around the corner of the Rest and Information Area.

Cisco saw the first reaction of the five—*his* five—was panic, and, in truth, his own heart gave a leap, as well. What were Josip and Marina doing there, with all those members of the Gypsyworld Assembly? From where he was, he couldn't hear what anybody said, but he was able, right away, to read his parents' body language, and their smiles. And, as he watched, the kids relaxed and dropped their bikes and started dancing all around, and hugging one another. Seconds later, Brenda turned and faced the woods, the place where she'd just come from.

Then he was running, running, running, with Duffy at his heels.

Julian F. Thompson

is the author of *The Grounding of Group 6, Simon Pure, A Band of Angels* (an ALA Best Book for Young Adults), and seven other books for young adults. He spent many years as a teacher—at a prep school, an alternative school, and at a minischool for suspended students, run out of a basement in Trenton, New Jersey.

He has been a writer all his life.

Julian Thompson lives with his wife, artist Polly Thompson, in Vermont.